The Sheikh's Girlfriend

Kate Goldman

The Sheikh's Girlfriend

Published by Kate Goldman

Copyright © 2019 by Kate Goldman

ISBN 978-1-07400-403-3

First printing, 2019

All rights reserved. No part of this book may be reproduced in any form or by any electronic or mechanical means including information storage and retrieval systems – except in the case of brief quotations in articles or reviews – without the permission in writing from its publisher, Kate Goldman.

www.KateGoldmanBooks.com

PRINTED IN THE UNITED STATES OF AMERICA

Dedication

I want to dedicate this book to my beloved husband, who makes every day in my life worthwhile. Thank you for believing in me when nobody else does, giving me encouragement when I need it the most, and loving me simply for being myself.

Table of Contents

CHAPTER 1 1

CHAPTER 2 7

CHAPTER 3 13

CHAPTER 4 20

CHAPTER 5 27

CHAPTER 6 36

CHAPTER 7 44

CHAPTER 8 51

CHAPTER 9 57

CHAPTER 10 64

CHAPTER 11 71

CHAPTER 12 79

CHAPTER 13 87

CHAPTER 14 94

CHAPTER 15 100

CHAPTER 16 107

CHAPTER 17 114

EPILOGUE 122

ABOUT KATE GOLDMAN 124

ONE LAST THING...125

Chapter 1

Tara coughed from all the dust and sand in her mouth. She looked outside and saw nothing but sand; they were in the middle of the desert. She turned to her left to see if her sister Tami was alright. The two of them had flown from the U.S. for a holiday in Omani. It was Tara's graduation present to Tami. Her younger sister had just graduated with an accounting degree. She was so proud of her. They had no one but each other. Their father died when their mother was pregnant with Tami. Their mother had passed a few years ago.

"Tami, are you okay?" Tara asked her sister who was still sitting next to her. The plane had just taken a rough landing.

"I am okay," Tami replied.

Tara looked around the plane, some of the passengers were injured but it did not seem like anything fatal. Tara tried to unbuckle her seatbelt but it seemed jammed. She swore under her breath as she tried to set herself free. "Tara, look," Tami said, pointing at the front of the plane. Tara looked in the direction her sister was pointing, she saw a group of men entering the plane. They were dressed in black clothes and red head scarves.

The Sheikh's Girlfriend

"Nomads," Tara said to Tami. She had read about them but never seen them in real life. "They must be here to help," she added.

The men stood at the entrance scanning around. The passengers were calling out for them to help. One man spoke in Arabic and jerked his head to the side. The other nomads started searching the passengers and taking their valuable things. The passengers were asking them why they were taking their things but the nomads did not reply.

Tara gasped when she realized that the nomads had weapons on their waists. They had swords and knives. She immediately felt scared. This did not seem like a good situation. No one knew what they would or could do. What was the reason for them to carry such weapons?

Some of the nomads cut the seatbelts, releasing the female passengers. They carried them out of the plane. Any man that tried to help was either kicked or punched. Tara noticed that they were taking the younger women. "They're kidnapping women," Tami said and immediately got into panic mode. Tara held her hand. She wanted to tell her to calm down and that everything was going to be okay but she too was frightened. She had no idea if they were going to be okay, she had no idea what was happening or why.

Tara looked through the window. There were plenty of horses outside. She figured that they had come on

The Sheikh's Girlfriend

horseback. One of the nomads approached Tara and Tami. He immediately started searching them. "Take what you want but please leave us alone," Tara said. The man looked up at Tara and saw her necklace. He ripped it off her neck. Tara screamed for him to return it to her. It was the only thing her mother left her.

The man who gave the orders at the beginning shouted something to the nomad that had taken Tara's necklace. He quickly nodded and cut Tami's seatbelt. Tami started screaming for him to put her down. Tara held onto Tami's hand and screamed for him to leave her. He shouted something in Arabic. "Please let her go or take both of us," Tara pleaded with him. He slapped Tara as she was not releasing her sister's hand, then picked Tami up and ran out of the plane with her.

Tara tried desperately to get out of her seatbelt. She groaned loudly with anger and frustration when she could not get out of it. The nomads ran out of the plane. Tara could see them through the window. They got on their horses and rode off. The female passengers they had taken, including Tami, were forced onto the horses with the nomads. Tara started crying for her sister. She did not know why Tami had been taken or if she was ever going to see her again.

Not long after, a few jeeps drove up and parked up beside the plane. A group of Middle Eastern men

The Sheikh's Girlfriend

jumped out. Tara creased her eyebrows. More men? she asked herself. Were they coming to kidnap the rest of them? It seemed that the nomads had taken the female passengers that appeared to be in their early twenties. The men from the jeep got on the plane. The passengers immediately started screaming and shouting.

"Please do not panic. We are here to help," one of them said. He was very tall and muscular. He had jet-black hair and a day-old beard. He said something in Arabic. The other men went to the passengers and helped them out of their seats.

Tara hesitated at first when one of them approached her. He looked at her and nodded, as if to ask her to trust him. She let him help her out and he helped her into the jeeps along with other passengers. "We help," he said to them and nodded. He returned to the plane to help the remaining passengers.

Some of the men drove the passengers to a campsite and returned to get the rest of the passengers. Other men stayed guarding the plane. They had to take a few trips until all of the passengers were safely evacuated from the plane.

The campsite they were taken to had plenty of tents set up. There were plenty of people there and some horses. The injured passengers were receiving medical attention. Luckily no one was badly injured. The injuries were all minor cuts and bruises from when

The Sheikh's Girlfriend

the plane crash-landed. Tara stood there holding herself, gazing at the area. Was she really safe there? she asked herself. She decided to find the man that came on the plane first and spoke. He seemed to be the one in charge.

Tara started regretting the trip. It was her idea to go somewhere interesting and exciting. She really wanted to do something for her sister's graduation. She did not want it to be an ordinary gift or dinner. She saved up her money and paid for the trip. Tami was excited about it. She was really happy. The two of them had never been outside the U.S. This was their first trip and then this happened.

Tara finally found the man after searching for a while. The campsite was pretty massive. He had been standing with other men speaking in Arabic. "Excuse me, please," Tara said as she ran her hand through her hair. They all stopped talking and looked at her.

"Yes?" the man replied. His voice seemed much deeper and more relaxed this time. He was quite tall. Tara had to look up while she spoke to him.

"Thank you for helping us," Tara said.

"It's fine," the man nodded. Tara sighed as she fought back the tears.

"Some passengers were kidnapped." She wanted to ask him so many things. She was not sure where to start.

"I am aware. We have been having issues with those nomads for a while."

"Are we safe here?"

"Yes."

Tara wanted to believe him. She silently prayed that they were safe. "What about the passengers that were taken, will they be okay?"

He was not sure how to reply to her. Those nomads had been causing problems in the desert for a while. They mostly robbed people but on some occasions they kidnapped women. He was not sure for what reason. "I hope so, we will do our best to find them."

Tara wanted a more reassuring answer but if they had been having issues with them for a while then it did not seem good. She just nodded. "Okay," she said. Her voice went as small as a child's. She was trying her best not to cry.

"Someone you know was taken?"

"My younger sister."

He nodded and expressed his sympathy. He told her once more that he was going to do his best to reunite them. Tara nodded and walked off. The tears were really burning her eyes. She never cried in front of people, so she held them in until she was away from him.

Chapter 2

Tara just stared at her plate. Although she was hungry she simply could not eat. The few English-speaking men had gathered up the passengers and given them food. There were lots of tents, pots, pans, food and even toiletries. Tara found it interesting that they had all these things in the desert. The food had been cooked over a fire. She had never been in the desert and it was fascinating to her.

Growing up, Tara and Tami always wanted to travel but they had never the opportunity. They would talk about all the exotic places they had always wanted to go to. Omani was one of those places they listed. It was not as famous as Dubai but it was still great and more affordable. It had beautiful beaches with white sands and clear water. There were so many tourist attractions.

"Eat," one of the men said as he was passing Tara. He had noticed that she was not eating. Tara looked up. He smiled and nodded at her. She smiled back and started eating. They had been served grilled strips of meat, vegetables and pita bread. The food tasted better than she had thought. Tami would have liked that; camping in the desert and eating Arabic food, Tara thought to herself. It was messed up that she was experiencing it due to the plane crash and the kidnapping.

After dinner, the passengers were given tents to sleep in. They had to share because they were more passengers than there were tents. Tara ended up sharing with four other women. One of them looked like she was in her mid-twenties and the other three looked to be above thirty. Tara got in her sleeping bag and immediately got into a fetal position.

"What is your name?" one of the women asked her.

"Tara," she replied.

That woman introduced herself as Emily, the others as Mandy, Hae-Na and Jackie. Hae-Na was the one in her mid-twenties. She was Korean-American. Mandy and Emily were both in their thirties. Jackie was the eldest. She was in her early forties.

It was a bad day for all them. No one had been expecting anything like that to happen. It was bad enough the plane crash-landed, the nomads did not have to rob them and kidnap people. Fortunately they all still had some belongings left, mainly clothes and shoes. The nomads had been aiming for things of value like jewelry and money.

***

The next morning, Tara was up and out of the tent very early. It was always difficult for her to sleep in a new environment, also the thought of her sister kept

The Sheikh's Girlfriend

her from finding any sleep. She was too worried about what was going to happen to her. She could only pray that her sister was safe.

Tara ran into the leader of the men that had rescued them from the crash site. "You are up early," he said to her. Tara nodded and asked him for his name. She at least needed to know what to call him. He said his name was Sofian. For a moment he studied Tara.

She was much shorter than he was. She had long, thick, wavy blonde hair, a small round nose and medium-sized lips. Her skin was a golden color. She wore a t-shirt and jeans. Tara's hourglass figure was very apparent. Sofian was used to very slender Middle Eastern women. Even though he had been abroad, he had always preferred Omani women. He found Tara's appearance intriguing though.

"I'm Tara," she said. He had not asked for her name but she gave it anyway. "So what is going to happen next? How long will we stay here?" she asked.

"We have to evacuate to Wella City as soon as more transportation has arrived."

"Wella City?"

"It is the closest city from here."

"Is it in the desert?" she asked him. He nodded in response. A city in the desert? Tara asked herself. Sounded interesting. Tami would have loved that sort of thing. Tara sighed.

The Sheikh's Girlfriend

Well, there were plenty of people there: the passengers and the Arabic men. They would run out of supplies soon. Also there was nowhere for them to wash. It made sense for them to evacuate to a different location. Tara noticed that Sofian spoke English fluently. The other men were not so fluent in their speech and the ones that were, had heavy accents. It made her curious about Sofian's background.

"How far are we from the city?" Tara asked.

"Four hours' drive."

Tara raised her eyebrows. That was close? It made her wonder just how far they were from Iqbal City, the capital. This drive to Wella City was long. She did not like long journeys. She always got bored easily. She was that kind of person that needed to be stimulated all the time. "And where will we stay?" she asked him. She was curious about where they would stay and if the government was going to get involved. She wondered if they were going to help the passengers.

Sofian narrowed his gaze at her. She asked a lot of questions. He tried to be patient because of her situation. However normally he would have already ended the conversation. He was not really a patient man. He was not used to random people questioning or even talking to him. They never got the opportunity anyway.

The Sheikh's Girlfriend

"I have arranged for accommodation. Do not worry." He turned on his heel to go. Tara frowned. Was he really walking off in the middle of a conversation? How rude was that? She just took a deep breath and let him go. Maybe she gave the impression that she was done speaking. Nevertheless she was not going to let it go that easily if he did that again. She hoped that he would not. He was their knight in a shining armor, she did not want to argue with him and seem ungrateful.

Hours later, after everyone was awake, they were served breakfast. Tara was happy to indulge in a hot cup of coffee. That was the only American thing that she had gotten so far. It reminded her of home, their two-bedroom apartment in the Bronx. Every morning, Tara woke up and had a cup of coffee and stood at her window watching people go by.

She sat with her tent mates, watching everyone at the campsite. She watched Middle Eastern men serve the passengers their breakfast. Even if the passengers did not like it, they had to eat it. They had no other option as they became dependent on these strangers. Tara watched Sofian walking towards the group of the men that were standing together. He was so tall and his step was part authoritative, part conceited.

He spoke to the men. They bowed their heads before they left. Tara raised an eyebrow. That was confirmation that he was the leader but why the head bow? Was that a sign of respect or was he a sheikh? Tami was the one who had taught her about sheikhs. She had all the Middle Eastern customs down. She was already interested their lifestyle and tradition. She probably would know if Sofian was a sheikh. Tara was clueless.

That was why this trip had been an amazing graduation gift for Tami. She had always wanted to go to a Middle Eastern country. She definitely wanted to meet a sheikh. Tara's thoughts were interrupted by the sounds of car engines. She turned her head towards the direction of the noise. She saw a lot of jeeps driving towards them.

After the jeeps parked up, the passengers were told that they would go to Wella City. Tara was able to get in the same jeep as her tent mates. She was happy because she had gotten acquainted with them. Their luggage was packed into the trunk of the car. The drive was very long. Tara felt like it was longer than four hours. She could not wait to get to the city. She always got restless easily. In the first part of the journey, the five of them were speaking. Then they just stopped speaking and went into their own worlds.

Chapter 3

Wella City was gated and guarded. The stone walls were very high. The stone roads were surprisingly in great condition. They drove past a market. There were lots of people selling different things. They stared at the jeeps going past with all the foreigners. They finally drove into a large compound and parked up. The compound was like a small gated community. All the passengers were asked to get out of the car as they had reached their destination.

The few passengers that had not been robbed and had no one missing were escorted to a different section. They were going to be taken to the capital city the next day so that they could either return to the U.S. or continue their vacations. Some of them were Omanians returning to their country.

The rest of the passengers were greeted by a well-dressed woman who spoke fluent English. She introduced herself as Mariam. She took them to their accommodation.

The buildings were rather interesting. They were made out of stone. The ones that were near the entrance were made out of sand-colored stone with dome-shaped roofs. The houses that the passengers were staying at were different. They were made out of brown stones arranged in a mosaic pattern. The windowsills and doorframes were made out of brown wood. Tara's jaw dropped to the ground when they walked inside the house. It was very modern on the inside. From the outside, you would not expect it to be. The floors were made out of tiles with intricate designs on them.

"What is this place?" Tara asked Mariam. She was too curious, she had to ask.

"This building was specially made for people traveling in the desert that needed a place to stay or for people that had lost their way," she replied.

"It's very nice."

"It is indeed. Right, we are here. This is where you all will be staying for the time being. Each room accommodates two people. So you may choose with whom you wish to share. Supper will be served at 7 p.m. Some members of the staff will come and escort you to the dining area," Mariam said before she left.

The bedrooms were located in a hallway like in hotels. Only this hallway was very wide and the walls were made of stones. The doorframes were wooden. Tara and Hae-Na shared a room since they were around the same age.

"This place is nice," Tara said as they walked into their room. There were two double beds in the bedroom. The room felt cool. It was air-conditioned. It also had large windows. Tara walked to the

The Sheikh's Girlfriend

windows to see the view. There was a stone pathway with palm trees along the edge, leading to a little fountain.

"I agree," Hae-Na said as she put her suitcase on the floor. Tara laid on the bed. It was comfortable. She smiled to herself. "I could just fall asleep right away," she added.

"Tell me about it." Hae-Na got into bed also. It was nice to be in a bed once again. Sleeping in a tent in the middle of the desert was not easy.

Tara faced Hae-Na and leaned her back against the window. "My sister and I used to share a room when we were younger," she said to Hae-Na.

"What is your sister like?" she asked Tara.

"Much more adventurous than I. She would really like this place."

"Don't you?"

"I do but she would have had her camera out taking pictures. She would want to know everything about the place." Tara laughed a little. "I think I am starting to be a little more like her," she added.

Hae-Na smiled at Tara. "Of course you would be. How old is she?"

"She is twenty-one. What made you want to come to this country?"

The Sheikh's Girlfriend

"To meet a sheikh."

Tara and Hae-Na both laughed. "Something Tami would say," Tara said.

Hae-Na smiled and told her that she was there on vacation also. She was traveling with her friend who had suggested it, and now she had been kidnapped.

Later that night, some of the workers went to summon the passengers for supper. The passengers followed them to the dining area. It was kind of nice. The setting was just like a restaurant. There were also tables outside, you could dine on the patio. Tara sat with her ex-tent mates.

***

The next day, after breakfast, Mariam showed the passengers around the place and at the end of the tour she took them to a separate building which had great facilities. That building was made for citizens of the city to use and also for the guests that stayed there. There was a library for those that wished to read. There was a recreation center where different types of sports and activities were available. Mariam told the passengers that they were welcome to use any of the facilities if they wished to.

After the tour, Tara decided to go for a walk and acquaint herself with the new environment. She especially wanted to go to the fountain she had seen from her room. It was only about 11 a.m. and it was already so hot. She was wearing wide-leg slacks and a tee shirt, but she felt like she was wearing too much. Tara came to a halt when she saw Sofian walking towards her.

"Morning," she greeted him.

"Morning," he said and kept on walking. Tara frowned and followed him.

"Do you live here too?" she asked. Dumb question, she thought to herself but she was actually curious. Also it was an opening for conversation.

"Yes," he replied. Although he lived mainly in Iqbal City, he spent a lot of time in Wella City. He had a feeling that if he told her, she would only ask further questions.

"How old is this city?"

Sofian narrowed his gaze. "Two hundred years," he replied reluctantly.

"Oh, that's old. Obviously it had to be refurbished and stuff but still it's quite old." Sofian just grunted in response. "I need to take pictures for my sister. She is really going to love it."

"Hmm." Admittedly he was not a people person. He had no idea what he was meant to say to that.

"What do the nomads do with their hostages?" Tara dreaded the answer to that question but she had to ask.

The Sheikh's Girlfriend

"I cannot guess." He was sure she had asked him something similar previously.

Tara sighed. "How often does something like this happen? I mean this doesn't happen all the time, right? It's not right."

Sofian stopped walking. He could hear from her voice that she was worried. "Not often," he said to her. Tara just nodded. "Any more questions?" he asked her.

"Not for now." Tara awkwardly scratched her neck. She stood there watching him walking away. She felt that he was kind of rude when he asked her if she had any more questions.

She turned on her heel and headed back to the house. Tara wondered if she had asked too many questions as she walked. Well, it was not her fault, anyone in that situation would have questions.

"Where did you go?" Hae-Na asked Tara when she walked back into the bedroom.

"Wanted to see the area," Tara replied as she threw herself on the bed.

"Did you?"

"Not really."

Hae-Na laughed a little bit. "What happened?"

The Sheikh's Girlfriend

Tara groaned before she replied. "I ran into one of the men that helped us. Struck up a conversation but apparently I was asking too much."

"Were you?" Hae-Na raised her eyebrows.

"Not really. I just think it's his nature to be cold. Never mind anyway. Where did you live back in the States?" There was not much point in talking about Sofian. Tara just had to make a mental note to not ask him so many questions next time.

"Manhattan," Hae-Na replied.

"Really?" Tara's eyes flew open. She quickly sat up. "It's such a small world. I'm from the Bronx."

"What? Oh my God!"

The two of them just started talking about their lives in New York. They talked about their favorite places to go and things to do. It was strange that although Tara and Hae-Na were from the same city and boarded the same plane, they were getting to know each other thousands miles away from the USA in the middle of the desert.

Chapter 4

Sofian was in his office trying to come up with a new strategy regarding the nomads. He had been tracking them for a few months. They started off robbing people, and then recently they started kidnapping women. Particularly those between sixteen and twenty-one. Sofian dreaded to think what the reason might be. It made him feel very uneasy. He needed to get ahold of the situation before it amplified.

"Sheikh," Amir said as he walked into Sofian's office. Amir had worked under Sofian for years, and was also his friend. Sofian looked up from his table.

"Amir, welcome, sit," Sofian said. Amir joined him at his desk. Amir had a map in his hands. He put it on the table and opened it.

"These marked areas are the ones where there have been incidences. It will be good to keep them under surveillance."

Sofian nodded. "If they know we are watching them, they might not make a move."

"What do you suggest?"

"An ambush."

"That can only work if we know if they are definitely going to make a move."

The Sheikh's Girlfriend

"Exactly." Sofian leaned back in his seat. They continued discussing ways to apprehend the nomads and find their location. They needed to put an end to all of it. Sofian's secretary knocked on the door before she entered his office. She brought with her a tray of refreshments. She placed it on the table.

"Anything else I can get you, sheikh?" She asked.

"No," Sofian replied without making eye contact with her. His focus was still on the maps. She bowed her head and left his office. Amir chuckled.

"You are going to break a lot of hearts when you settle down," Amir joked. Sofian looked up.

"Where is this coming from?"

"You did not see the way she was looking at you?"

"I did not. Besides, who says I am going to settle down?"

"Your mother."

Sofian grunted and took a glass of cold drink from the tray. His mother had been asking him to settle down for a while. He was the only of his siblings that had not married. His mother was very persistent. Sofian was not keen on the idea of marriage. He liked the way he lived. He ignored her every time she brought it up.

"Well, not any time soon," Sofian said.

The Sheikh's Girlfriend

Amir smiled and started eating some almonds from the tray. He asked Sofian about the passengers. He had not been with Sofian when he rescued them from the crash site. Sofian answered Amir's question. As he was talking, Tara popped up in his mind. He made a face. She was an interesting character; very inquisitive, odd dress sense, interesting figure. He dismissed the thoughts of her and continued speaking about the situation regarding the passengers.

***

The passengers were served some traditional Middle Eastern foods. There was rice and spicy minced lamb stuffed in grape leaves sprinkled with some lemon juice. There was also some freshly baked pita bread and a salad with cucumbers, chickpeas, spring onions, tomatoes, feta cheese cubes and some herbs. Tara took her time eating the food. "The taste is interesting," Tara said.

"I agree, I am loving this salad," Hae-Na replied. Tara wiggled her eyebrows in response.

"I indulge in Middle Eastern cuisines from time to time," Emily said.

"Oh really?"

"Yes, I love it."

Tara was sitting with her ex-tent mates. The five of them just bonded after sharing a tent. They discussed their favorite cuisines that they enjoyed back in the

The Sheikh's Girlfriend

States. During the conversation, Tara noticed Sofian walking into the dining area with two other men and Mariam. The four of them sat at a table. Immediately after, the waitresses served them their dinner. They smiled and bowed their heads just before they left. Tara frowned to herself. It made her curious why they were bowing their heads.

"Tara?" Mandy called out.

"Yes?" Tara had been focused on Sofian, she had zoned out of the conversation.

"Do you have a boyfriend?" Mandy asked her.

"No." Tara had been single for a while now. Her sister and friends teased her about it.

"How about you?" Mandy asked Emily. The conversation had turned to relationships when Mandy began talking about her ex-husband. This trip was a treat to herself because she had just finalized the divorce. The marriage had come to an end because of his infidelity.

"I am engaged," Emily said.

"Aww," all the ladies said at once. Emily looked at the empty ring finger on her left hand.

"The nomads took my ring."

"Oh no," Mandy said.

"That is sad," Jackie added. Emily sighed.

"My fiancé worked very hard to get me that ring. He got it for me three months after proposing," Emily said. Tara placed her hand on her heart.

"That is awful," Hae-Na said.

"I really hope these evil nomads get arrested soon," Tara said.

A waitress came to clear their table as they were finished eating. They thanked her as she took the plates away. Mandy suggested that they all go for a walk together. No one had any objections. They all stood up and followed her out. As they were walking out, they passed Sofian. He made eye contact with Tara.

She was not sure of what to do. Was she meant to smile at him or what? Instead she just held his gaze. She felt a little awkward. Fortunately for her, his colleagues were deep in conversation, so no one noticed her. She sighed with relief when she stepped out into the cool air. That eye contact was awkward and tense.

Tara breathed in the fresh air. It was really hot during the day but the temperature dropped during the night. It became warm with a cool breeze. "I like the weather like this," Tara said with a smile on her face. Hae-Na agreed with her. She loved late-night walks.

The five of them walked around the compound. It was very big. Each building was made out of stone,

The Sheikh's Girlfriend

but was made slightly different from the others. Each building had its own uniqueness. "I love the architecture," Jackie said.

"Yes ma'am, the buildings are interestingly built," Emily agreed.

"Just the fact that all of this is in the middle of the desert amazes me," Tara said. She was still wrapping her head around the whole ordeal. "Wait for me, I need to get my camera," she added. She wanted to take pictures of everything so that she could show her sister.

"Okay, we will wait," Mandy replied.

Tara ran back towards the building. She came to a halt when she bumped into something. She staggered backwards a little. She looked up and saw Sofian standing there. Tara rubbed the back of her neck awkwardly. "Sorry," she said.

"Where is the fire?" he asked her. He spoke so calmly with a blank expression on his face.

"I was going to get my camera."

Sofian creased his eyebrows. He was not even going to ask. He just nodded and began to walk away. "Hey!" Tara called out to him. She had just remembered something she wanted to ask him about. He stopped and turned to look at her. No one had ever said "Hey" to him. They always referred to him in a more respectful way.

"Why did the waitresses bow to you? It was to you, right?" she asked.

He just stood there looking at her. Was she really asking him that? "I wonder," he replied sardonically. The fact that she did not know his identity made him not bother to tell her. She should have known that already. But then again she was Western, the ones that did not pay attention to the news would not know him.

"Are you like a sheikh or something?"

She had begun with all the questions. "Something," he replied.

Tara narrowed her gaze at him. "You are kind of rude," she said. She felt ungrateful saying that to someone who had rescued her from the terrible situation she was in. However, he was rude and she had to call him out on it. He did not even seem bothered by what she had just said. He just shrugged his shoulders and walked off. Tara was left speechless with her jaw hanging open. She could not believe that he had not responded. She groaned in irritation and walked off.

Chapter 5

Tara returned to the other ladies with her camera. They walked around the compound seeing the place and just talking. Tara was trying to take pictures but she was distracted by thoughts of Sofian. She barely knew him and he was already rubbing her the wrong way. He was very unfriendly and rude. When he answered her questions, it was as if he did not want to. The last conversation was the one that showed his rudeness. He refused to tell her his identity, not that it mattered, but he worsened the situation when he walked away.

"Tara, are you still with us?" Hae-Na asked.

"Yes, I am. I was just admiring the sky," Tara replied. The sun had set, so the sky was a pale pink and blue color.

"I know, it's beautiful."

"Can we leave the compound to go see the markets?" Mandy asked.

"Of course we should be able to," Jackie replied.

"It would be so nice to see the markets," Tara said. "Let's go tomorrow"

The Sheikh's Girlfriend

They all agreed to go sometime after breakfast. It was better to go before midday, before it got really hot. They returned back to their rooms.

***

Right after breakfast, Tara and the other four ladies headed for the market. Finding it was not as easy as they had hoped it to be. The place they were staying at was extremely large. It took them a while to find the exit. "This is frustrating," Hae-Na complained. Tara laughed in response. She was never good with directions, maps, things like that. She always got lost. So when they had decided to go to the market, she decided not to volunteer ideas. She just followed quietly.

"I do not even know where to go, so I cannot help," Tara said. The other ladies were trying to figure out where to go. Tara noticed a man walking past. She ran towards him to ask for directions. "Excuse me, hi," she said.

"Hello." He smiled at her.

"Hi, we are trying to get to the market. How do we get out of this place? We have been at it for a while now."

He smiled at her again. "It is a large place," he said.

"Oh, tell me about it. I think I have lost a couple of pounds from all this walking." The man laughed a little. Tara smiled and introduced herself. He

The Sheikh's Girlfriend

introduced himself as Amir. Tara immediately asked herself why Sofian was not that receptive.

Amir escorted the ladies out of the estate. Tara was grateful because if he had given directions, she would have gotten lost. Amir spoke to them as he walked with them. He just asked simple questions like how they were finding the place and the food. He parted ways with them when they reached the gates.

"He's very handsome," Hae-Na said as she watched him walk away.

"Very," Emily agreed.

The five of them walked down dusty stone roads. The people looked at them as they walked past. They reached the market shortly after. It was very busy at the market. There were so many stalls. So many things were being sold; clothes, jewelry, sweets. Tara whipped out her camera and started taking pictures.

They went to a stall that sold pastries and sweets. The woman at the stall was inviting them over to try some pastries. They first tried *basbousa*, which was a cake baked from semolina with an almond in the middle. Hae-Na and Tara loved it. They both had a sweet tooth.

"Where are you from?" the woman running the stall asked.

"America," Emily replied.

The woman smiled. "We rarely get tourists here," she said.

"I would imagine so. This city is right in the middle of the desert. Have you lived here all your life?" Tara asked.

"Yes."

Her accent was very heavy but her English was good. The other people in the market did not speak English. Hae-Na pulled some money out of her wallet and bought some sweets and pastries. Fortunately her money had not been stolen.

"Your English is very good," Mandy said to the woman. The woman smiled at Mandy.

"When the prince came to rebuild the city, he also provided more learning opportunities," she said.

"The prince?" Hae-Na asked.

"Yes, the youngest one."

Another woman approached the stall and said something to her in Arabic. "Well, we will leave you to it. Thank you," Jackie said. All five of them smiled at her and bid her farewell.

"The prince, huh," Emily said as she stared upwards blissfully. She had never met a prince before. Back in the U.S., there was no royal family.

The Sheikh's Girlfriend

"It is amazing that a prince would put so much effort into such a small city," Tara said. She was impressed. She saw princes as just rich people and rich people usually did not care about anyone but themselves. It was nice to learn that the princes in Omani were different, not that she had ever met any princes.

"I concur. These little cities are the ones that are normally ignored or forgotten about," Jackie said.

They kept looking at stuff in the market and buying stuff. They decided to head back when it got hotter. The desert sun was very hot. They just wanted to get back and sit in the shade.

***

A few days later, Tara could not get to sleep, so she decided to go for a walk. She was still so worried about her sister. The market had taken her mind off her sister but now she was really thinking about her. It had been almost a week since she was kidnapped. There had not been any news. She was getting worried.

During her walk she saw Sofian just when he drove his fist into a palm tree. Tara's eyes widened. She approached him, looked to him and asked, "What is going on?" Sofian turned his head and saw Tara standing there looking at him. He groaned with frustration. It was bad enough that he was having a hard time, now Tara was here probably with more questions.

"Sofian, are you okay?" Tara asked him.

"I am fine," he snapped. He turned on his heel to walk off, but Tara spoke before he could.

"You are not fine, otherwise why punch the tree?" Tara looked down at his hand. Some skin had come off. She took his hand and inspected the wound. She was used to caring for her little sister. She acted without thought, it was reflex. Sofian tried to snatch his hand back. "Stay still," she said. He grunted and looked off in the distance. He was not used to people just touching him, especially when he had not petitioned for it. He felt strange with Tara touching his hand. Her small hands were soft and warm.

"Not too much skin came off. Make sure to clean it and bandage it," Tara said as she let go of his large hand. Sofian looked at her and knit his eyebrows, he could look after himself. However he was amused at her telling him how to. "So what happened?" Tara asked.

"What happened where?" he asked.

"What is making you so angry?"

"Now is not the time." He sounded calmer than when she first approached him. Tara said nothing. She just stood there looking at him with concern.

The Sheikh's Girlfriend

He looked at her, she did not look like she was going to leave. He sighed with frustration. "More people were robbed," he said. Tara raised her eyebrows.

"By the nomads?" Tara breathed.

"Yes."

"That is terrible." Tara placed her hands on her stomach. Sofian ran his hand through his hair. "Was there anyone kidnapped or hurt?"

"Fortunately not."

"These people were traveling or what?"

"Traveling, I guess"

"Tourists or Omanians?"

"Does it matter?" Sofian was getting more annoyed because of her numerous questions.

"Not really!" she spat out in fury. Even after kidnapping her sister and many others, they were not satisfied. She found it very upsetting. These nomads needed to be caught pronto. "I wish those men would get caught already!" Tara voiced out in frustration. The sooner they got caught, the sooner she could get her sister back.

"We have been doing everything we could," Sofian snapped. He felt as though she had accused them of not trying hard enough. He was already getting defensive.

"I never said you were not." Tara placed her hands on her hips. She did not appreciate being snapped at like that. Sofian punched the tree once more. "Stop that! Punching the tree does not help anything," she said to him.

"Talking to you will not help either."

"You need to calm down."

He grunted. She was right. He needed to regain his composure. He was just so annoyed and frustrated. He had been doing his best trying to find these nomads but was never able to. "Why are you out here anyway?" he asked her. It was night time, she should have been sleeping instead of walking around by herself.

"I could not sleep, so I came out for a walk."

"That will not help you sleep."

"No, but it will take my mind off Tami." Sofian creased his eyebrows. "My younger sister."

"Oh."

"I am sure you will find a way to apprehend those nomads. Fighting the tree will not do you any good, you will only just hurt your hand." Tara turned away and left. This time she was the one to walk away. Sofian was always the one to walk off before the end of a conversation. She decided to get back inside. It seemed impossible to have a decent conversation with Sofian.

Chapter 6

The next morning, Tara was filling Hae-Na in on the fact the nomads were still robbing people. Hae-Na was very disappointed to hear that. She too wanted them to get caught quickly. She wanted to have her friend back. She was filled with worry every single day. She was fortunate to have met Tara, otherwise she would not able to cope. Tara and the other ladies helped to divert her thoughts from her missing friend.

Tara and Hae-Na finished getting ready and headed for breakfast. Jackie, Mandy and Emily were already there waiting for them. Hae-Na and Tara greeted the others as they sat down. Moments later, the waitress brought them their breakfast. That day, they were having breakfast on the veranda. Some of the passengers were dining inside and some were outside.

"The service in this place is really great," Jackie commented. She loved getting served great food. The place was run like a restaurant and it was so clean.

"Yes, I agree," Mandy added.

"I love the idea of eating outside," Tara said.

"I have never liked it. I always feel like something is going to fly into my food," Emily said. Hae-Na and Jackie laughed at her.

The Sheikh's Girlfriend

"Oh, it's that handsome…what was his name again?" Hae-Na pointed out. They all turned to see who she was talking about.

"Amir," Tara said. She noticed that he was walking with Sofian. They were talking about something. Tara wondered if they were discussing the nomads. She had the urge to go and ask but she suppressed it. Some women were walking towards him and Amir. They stopped and bowed their heads. They were looking at him smiling before they walked off.

"Who is the other man?" Emily asked.

"I remember him in the plane," Hae-Na said and creased her eyebrows.

"Sofian," Tara said with obvious displeasure in her voice.

"What has he done to you?" Hae-Na asked.

"He is handsome," Emily said.

"Very handsome," Mandy added.

"If I did not have a husband…" Jackie said, staring at him. Tara frowned. He was a hard man to speak with, he did not offer a warm reception but he was attractive and he had big strong hands. Mariam approached Amir and Sofian. She bowed to Sofian and started speaking to them. Even she looked at him with stars in her eyes. Tara rolled her eyes and kept eating her breakfast.

The Sheikh's Girlfriend

"Morning, ladies," a voice sounded moments later. Tara looked up and saw Amir looking at them smiling. Sofian had his usual expressionless face.

"Morning," all of them except Tara said to him at the same time. She was late in answering, since she had not seen him coming.

"How are you?" Tara asked with a smile on her face.

"I am well, thank you," he replied.

Amir and Sofian walked inside the dining room. Mariam had gone in a different direction from them. Sofian and Amir sat down in the dining room. "You know them?" Sofian asked Amir, referring to Tara and her friends.

"Not really, I just met them a few days ago. They were trying to go to the souk, well, they called it a market." Amir smiled. He remembered Tara's joke about losing pounds on the way to the market.

"Oh." Sofian narrowed his gaze. He guessed it was Tara that had approached Amir. She was the one with all the questions in the world.

"The blonde one with the golden tan asked me for directions. She said they had been lost. She seems rather charming."

Sofian raised his eyebrows. He was right that it was Tara that had approached him, but charming? He

The Sheikh's Girlfriend

must have been speaking about somebody else. She was something else but not charming.

"What is the matter?" Amir asked Sofian. He could tell from his facial expression that there was something on his mind. He had known him for a long time.

"She is not charming," Sofian replied and sipped his coffee.

"You have met?"

"Yes."

"And what happened?"

Sofian sighed before he replied. He was not really up to talking about Tara. "She is quite inquisitive and a little annoying."

Amir laughed. "I am sure she is not that bad. This is you we are talking about," he said.

"Excuse me?"

"Sheikh, you have to admit how particular you are with things. The slightest thing that is not your preference, you consider it a fault."

Sofian shrugged his shoulders. It was very true. He liked things a certain way and he had always gotten things the way he wanted them. He had never met a woman like Tara and did not know how to deal with her. He changed the subject and started talking about

The Sheikh's Girlfriend

the nomads. He was still very angry that they had struck again. They needed to come up with a new idea fast. He did not want any more innocent people to suffer at their hands.

Sofian told Amir to go meet the people that had been robbed by the nomads the day before. He was to take a few men and escort them to their destination and give them some sort of compensation for what they had lost.

Amir smiled and nodded. He liked working with Sofian. Even though he had such a cold exterior, he cared for the people. He even used his own money to look after them. He dined in the hall once or twice a week to make sure things were up to par. He wanted to know what they were being served and what the service was like. He was not like a normal sheikh. He did not simply take reports, he had to see for himself. Sofian was pretty hands-on.

"You will make some woman happy one day," Amir joked. Sofian looked up and narrowed his gaze at him. Amir laughed. He enjoyed laughing at him about that subject. Amir nodded at Tara and her friends as they walked through. They had just finished their breakfast and had to walk through the dining area in order to return to their rooms.

Tara elbowed Hae-Na to get her attention. She was staring at Amir. "Do you need a bucket for your

The Sheikh's Girlfriend

drool?" Tara said to Hae-Na jokingly. Emily laughed. She too had noticed Hae-Na staring.

"He is too handsome," Hae-Na said.

"I do not blame you, honey," Emily said.

They all headed up to Jackie's room. She was the only one not sharing, because there were five of them. She was also the eldest, so it was more fitting for her to be in a room by herself. When they got into her room, she showed them pictures of her daughter.

"She is beautiful," Mandy commented. The others also agreed.

"Her name is Stacy," Jackie replied with a small smile and tucked a chestnut lock of hair behind her ear. She missed her daughter. "We were traveling here to see her grandmother, she added. Jackie's husband was Omanian. Most of his family still lived in Omani.

"How old is she?" Emily asked.

"Eighteen."

"She is still a baby," Mandy said.

"So your husband is Omanian?" Tara asked. Jackie nodded. "He was not traveling with the two of you?"

"No," Jackie replied. He had business to take care of, so he had not been able to travel with them. His mother had been requesting to see Stacy, so they had finally decided to come and see her.

"How about you, Emily, what brought you to Omani?" Hae-Na asked.

"Well, it was meant to be my bachelorette trip," Emily replied. She was to get married in two weeks. So her friends organized a ladies' trip before she tied the knot. She was traveling with two of her friends, and both of them had been kidnapped.

"It would have been fun trip if the plane had not crashed," Jackie said. "I remember the first time I came out here, I loved it."

"It's so sad that this had to happen and ruin everything. On top of the trip being ruined, those bastards took my ring."

"I am so angry for you. All of things to steal, they had to take that," Tara said.

"They're heartless! I hope they are caught and punished severely," Hae-Na added. Tara touched her collarbone. It was so strange to have it empty. She was used to wearing her necklace. It made her angry that the nomads had taken it. They had taken the two things that mattered to her the most. She wished she could make them pay for what they did.

"Maybe one good thing will come out of all this for you," Emily said to Hae-Na.

Hae-Na made a face before she replied. "And what is that?" she asked.

The Sheikh's Girlfriend

"A handsome Arabic man." They all burst into laughter.

"Well, I would not mind," Hae-Na said and giggled. She had never met a man as good-looking as Amir.

Chapter 7

Tara was sitting by the fountain looking at pictures on her camera. She came across some pictures of herself with Tami at the airport before they boarded. Her little sister had a big smile on her face. She was so excited. Tears rolled down Tara's face. It had been more than a week now. She had never been away from Tami for that long. It was killing her.

Sofian slowed down when he saw Tara sitting by the fountain. She was everywhere. He saw her far more than he wanted. Normally he would want to avoid her but she looked upset. Part of him wanted to still avoid her but strangely there another part of him wanted to comfort her, even if he did not know how. He approached her slowly.

Sofian cleared his throat before he spoke. "Are you alright?" he asked her. Tara wiped her tears and looked up. She knitted her eyebrows when she saw Sofian standing there.

"I am okay," she replied. It shocked her that he had bothered to ask.

Well, I tried, Sofian thought to himself. He was not good with follow-up questions in such situations. The first answer was what he took. He was just about to walk away when she started talking. "Just missing my

The Sheikh's Girlfriend

sister," she said. Sofian looked at her. Tara handed him the camera. He took it from her and looked at the screen.

"How old is she?" Sofian asked.

"Twenty-one."

Sofian handed her back the camera. He could see she wanted to talk more and she looked so sad. He reluctantly sat down next to her. Tara put her hand in the water. It was cool and refreshing. "I have no other siblings," she said.

Sofian grunted in response. He did not know what to say to her. "Do you have any?" Tara asked him.

"Two brothers," he replied.

"Older or younger?"

"Both older."

"Aww, you are the baby," Tara looked at Sofian. He raised his eyebrows at her. He was not quite sure what she was talking about. No one had ever referred to him as that. "What are they like?" She was curious to know if his brothers were the same as he was.

"Normal." He was not sure what to say. Most people were familiar with his family, so he never had to answer such questions. Tara frowned at him. Most people would have something to say about their siblings. Before she could make a complaint, Mariam approached them. She greeted Sofian with a bow.

The Sheikh's Girlfriend

"Excuse me, your highness, there is a message for you," Mariam said and handed him a note. Tara raised her eyebrows.

"Whose highness?" Tara asked. Sofian just opened the note and started reading it.

"I beg your pardon," Mariam said.

"You said 'your highness.'"

Mariam looked confused. Sofian folded the note and dismissed Mariam. She bowed her head before she left. Tara was looking at him wide-eyed. He rose to his feet. "Your highness?" she repeated. Sofian shrugged his shoulders.

"Try not to worry about your sister. We are going to find her," Sofian said and rubbed her shoulder before he walked off. Tara was left sitting there with her jaw hanging open. Was he a prince? she wondered to herself. It explained why he was rude, even though it was no excuse. But what was he doing out there?

Tara went to find the answers to her questions from Amir later that day. It was just before supper when she saw him walking outside. She ran from the dining room to catch up with him. He smiled and greeted her.

"Hi, how are you?" she greeted him.

"I am well, yourself?"

The Sheikh's Girlfriend

"I am fine." Tara cleared her throat. "So, Sofian is a prince?" she asked him. She knew she was too curious about things. That was why science was good for her, according to her mother. Growing up, Tara was always too curious about things. Her mother always said that she was going to be a scientist because of that curiosity.

Amir looked at Tara with his eyebrows raised. "Yes, the sheikh is a prince. You were not aware?" he replied.

"No. In the States we do not have any royal families, so all of this is new to me, but why is he out here? Shouldn't he be living in the palace somewhere?" she asked. Amir laughed. Sofian had warned him about her inquisitions.

"Well, he makes it his duty to man the desert and the cities in it."

Tara remembered the woman from the market. She had said that the prince rebuilt the city. Tara frowned to herself. Sofian did all that? Really? He did not suit the part. He had shown her a different side.

"So he was responsible for rebuilding this city and stuff?"

"Precisely. Besides being old, the city was not as residential as other cities. So he took upon himself to develop the city and provide necessary educational opportunities."

The Sheikh's Girlfriend

"Oh wow. How long did all this take?"

"Ten years."

Tara had the urge to ask him how old Sofian was but she decided not to. She had already asked him too many questions. "You have known him for that long?" She could not help but ask him that question.

"I have know the sheikh for more than ten years."

Tara nodded and thanked him for answering all her questions. He smiled and went on his way. Had it been Sofian, he would have ended the conversation a lot quicker. She returned to the dining room feeling rather puzzled. The prince they had been impressed by a few days ago at the market was the same man that frustrated her. How could he rebuild a city and not be able to hold a simple conversation? He was truly a strange character.

***

Amir was getting ready to ride out into the desert. He had gathered some of their men to go out into the desert to search for the nomads. There were some areas they had not covered yet. This time they were going to ride on horseback. It was quicker.

"So I had a conversation with the American lady," Amir said to Sofian. He was saddling up his horse. He stopped and stared at Amir with a blank facial expression.

The Sheikh's Girlfriend

"Tara," he said. It had to be her, no one else.

"And you say her name with such pleasure," Amir said sardonically. Sofian grunted in response. "She was not aware of your identity."

"Initially, I suspected that from the way she spoke to me. Then I confirmed it when she asked me if I was a sheikh or something."

Amir laughed. "I am guessing you did not tell her."

"I should not have to." Sofian got on his horse. Amir got on his also. "We need to return before dark."

Sofian rode off towards his men. He gave them instructions on what he wanted to accomplish. Afterwards, they rode out of the estate.

Hae-Na was standing at her window when she saw them riding off. "Amir looks so manly on horseback," she said to Tara.

"What?" Tara asked as she sat up. Hae-Na told Tara what she had just seen. She gave her a full description of what Amir was wearing. Tara just smiled and shook her head. "So it turns out Sofian is a prince," she said. Hae-Na rushed over to Tara wide-eyed.

Tara figured she had to tell her everything that had happened from the start. In those situations, Tara would usually share with her sister. In this case, she only had Hae-Na to tell. It was okay because she had bonded with her over the past week and a half. Tara told Hae-Na everything from the start.

"Oh, this is so exciting. He is a prince! It suits him," Hae-Na said. "He is so tall and handsome."

"And rude," Tara added.

"With a body like that, it is forgivable."

Tara burst into laughter. Hae-Na was reacting the way Tami would. "It is inexcusable," she said. Just because he was a prince, it did not mean that he could treat people however he wanted.

"Well, he seems to be doing good things with his post. He is not a spoiled prince that lives in the palace and sponges off the public's tax money."

"That is true."

"Do you like him?"

"What? No."

"Why not?"

Tara raised her eyebrows. Had she not made it clear enough that she was not a big fan of his personality? There was so much to dislike there. Yes, he was handsome and had an amazing body but that did not mean she had to like him. She just shrugged her shoulders and did not even bother to respond.

Chapter 8

Tara was sitting in the sun with Hae-Na looking at Sofian. She could not believe that he was a prince. It did not make a difference to her anyway. She had not changed the way she looked at him. Some of the passengers were loitering outside also. The women seemed to be taken by Sofian's presence. They watched him walking past them.

Amir approached Sofian. "Sheikh, we have two of the nomads in custody," Amir said as he approached the sheikh. He had not even bothered to bow to him. He was so eager to let him know the good news.

"What? How? Where did you apprehend them?" Sofian asked.

"In the desert."

Sofian frowned. "Take me there at once," he said. Amir nodded and led the way. He explained how they had found the nomads. They were on horseback in the middle of the desert. Amir had been riding out with some of the men as per Sofian's instruction. Fortunately they found the nomads riding together. They quickly arrested them and brought them back. Amir's men made sure there were not any others in sight.

The Sheikh's Girlfriend

The building where they were heading was well separated from the others. It was built out of stone with a dome-shaped roof just like the rest. They walked inside and down a stone staircase. The two nomads were being held in separate rooms. Sofian headed into one of them. There were two guards outside the room. They bowed to Sofian and opened the wooden doors. The sheikh walked in and saw the nomad sitting at a table.

Sofian joined him at the table. He analyzed him for a moment before he spoke. He sat down at the table in front of him. He stared at him and did not say anything. The nomad looked away. The sheikh had an intimidating gaze.

Sofian leaned forward. He did not even know where to start. He had so much he wanted to say to him. Finally he had seen the face of one of the nomads, the men that had caused so much strife and mayhem in the desert. "So you are one of them," Sofian said. It was taking him all he had to remain calm. The nomad did not say anything. He had been trained not to speak so easily but he was still intimidated by the sheikh.

"For months your people committed unpardonable crimes in my territory," Sofian said.

"I have no idea what you speak of," the nomad replied.

The Sheikh's Girlfriend

"Oh but you do. I will give you and your associate some time to give my men the location that you are holding the hostages. If you do not cooperate, well, you will live out the rest of your days eating from a tube."

The nomad swallowed nervously. Sofian never made empty threats. His reputation for sticking to his word and being so stern was well known. Not only was he a sheikh, he was the youngest prince of the country. It was never wise to cross him.

Sofian stood up and left the room. It was better that way. Amir was always the one to handle interrogations. Sofian was too short-tempered. It was surprising that he had not lunged towards him and grabbed his collar. "Get them to speak," Sofian ordered Amir.

"As you wish," Amir said and bowed his head.

***

Tara was starting to grow weary tired of her situation. She was starting to feel caged. There was not much to do. Her every day was exactly the same. She was on her millionth walk. She sometimes walked with Hae-Na and the other ladies but sometimes she walked alone as it cleared her mind. Jackie and Mandy were talking to one of the passengers. It was an older lady who was feeling sad about her granddaughter that had been kidnapped by the nomads. Hae-Na and Emily were back in their rooms.

Tara took an unfamiliar path. There were still areas she had not explored. The path she was walking on was nicer. There were neatly cut and evenly spaced palm trees on both sides of the pavement. There weren't any buildings around. There was only one large one at the end of the pavement. There were also guards around the building.

Suddenly she saw Sofian walking towards her. She had mixed feelings about seeing him. They usually had unpleasant exchanges, she hated to admit it but it was something that spiced up her day. He was a mysterious man. She was curious about him. Tara wanted to walk past him but he asked her what she was doing there.

"Just walking," Tara replied.

"You walk a lot," Sofian said sarcastically.

"Well, there is nothing else to do."

Sofian said nothing. He sometimes found her amusing. She started looking at him strangely, as if she was studying him. "What?" he asked her.

"You a prince, it explains some things but not all."

"What does it explain?"

The Sheikh's Girlfriend

Tara just made a sound. By saying what she thought, she would end up insulting him. "It does not explain why you are out in the middle of the desert," she said.

"I look after my people, what is wrong in that?"

"Nothing." Tara turned away to continue on her path.

Sofian made a face. This was the first time she had ever ended the conversation so quickly. She always had a ton of questions for him. He took her arm and pulled her back.

"What?" she cried out.

"That path leads to my home and you cannot go there."

Tara raised her eyebrows. It made sense why the place was guarded. It also had a different architecture from the other buildings. It was built on a lawn. It had two stories, and the roof was a flat rectangle shape unlike the roofs of the other buildings that were dome-shaped. On the left side, there was a stone staircase leading to a balcony above the first floor. There were pillars evenly spaced out, holding up the roof.

Tara was curious what the inside looked like but Sofian was definitely not going to show her and she was not going to ask. "Your house looks nice," she said.

The Sheikh's Girlfriend

"Thank you," he replied. He knew that she was going to ask about her sister or what was going on with the search for the nomads. He decided to beat her to the punch and tell her what was happening. Although he could just not tell her anything, he felt the need to tell her. "We have some nomads in custody," he said. Tara knitted her eyebrows.

"What?" she said. She could not believe her ears.

"I thought you should know."

"You caught some of them?"

"Just two, they have not said much but it is a step from where we were."

"It's a lead."

"We hope to get a location out of them."

At last there was a lead, there was some hope. Tara was not sure if she wanted to march over there and punch one of them in the face or jump up with joy. Instead she jumped on him. She did not think, she was just so happy to hear some good news. She just jumped on him and wrapped her arms around his neck.

Sofian was surprised by her reaction. He surprised himself by wrapping his arms around her waist. He held her tightly in his arms. Just for a while, he stood there holding her. She felt warm and comfortable. She smelled so nice.

Chapter 9

Realization sunk in. Tara was in Sofian's arms. She unwrapped her arms from his neck and got down. She was feeling awkward but not regretful. It felt good in his arms; comfortable, safe and strong. She tucked a wavy lock of blonde hair behind her ear. "Excuse me, just got a little carried away," she said.

Sofian grunted in response. He felt the urge to pull her into his embrace but he restrained himself. "I have to go," he said to her and walked off. Tara had her hands on her hips as she watched him walk away. He had actually dismissed himself before he walked off. He had not just walked off in the middle of the conversation like he normally did. Tara had also realized that his facial expression was warmer than usual.

Sofian went to his office and waited for Amir to bring him back a report about the nomads. The sheikh sat down at his desk. He had work of his own to complete but his mind was filled with thoughts of Tara. He remembered having her in his arms. It was a reaction he had not expected. It made him feel good to see her that happy. It made him want to find her sister sooner for her. Sofian could not understand himself.

"Sheikh," Amir said interrupting Sofian's thoughts as he walked into the room. Sofian turned to look at him and leaned forward.

"Yes, what happened?" Sofian asked.

"It took a lot but we finally got a location out of one of them."

"That is good news. Where is it?"

"El-Sadi."

Sofian raised his eyebrow. El-Sadi was small village lying on the border of Omani, just outside the desert. The village was not very populous. That was one of the areas they had not searched. They had not even thought of searching the village.

"It is well out of the desert, they must have a campsite somewhere in the desert," Sofian said. Because they were traveling on horseback, they could not make it out of the desert without having a rest; especially with hostages.

"Yes, they do. The same nomad that told us the location is willing to lead us to the campsite."

"He divulged the information rather quickly."

"Yes." Amir laughed. "The man was rather scared after you left him."

"It was that one," Sofian grunted in satisfaction. He knew his appearance had rattled the man, even though the nomad had tried not to appear intimidated.

"Your reputation never fails you."

"And yet there are others who are still unaware of it." Sofian was thinking of Tara. She was the only person that approached him so casually and even after she learned that he was a prince, she was still not intimidated by him.

The sheikh instructed Amir to send a few men to conduct surveillance of the location discreetly. They needed to find out how many nomads were there, what kind of weapons they had if they had weapons. Sofian had to be sure of what he was getting himself into before he rode out into the desert. Amir agreed with the sheikh. It was best to figure out the situation before taking any action.

***

The following day after breakfast, Tara debated with herself whether or not she should tell the others about the nomads being in custody. It would be good news for them but she did not want to get their hopes up if nothing came of it. She was trying not to get her hopes up high also but she could not help it. Suddenly the thought of her in Sofian's arms returned to her mind. Tara felt a little embarrassed about jumping into his arms like that. It surprised her that he had not pushed her away. Instead he embraced her.

"What are you thinking about so intently?" Emily asked Tara as she approached her. She sat down next to her on the concrete step outside the recreation center. The other ladies were playing table tennis inside with the other passengers.

"Nothing," Tara replied with a smile. She could not possibly tell Emily that she was thinking about Sofian. She could not even understand her thoughts yet.

"It did not look like nothing."

"Aren't you playing?"

"No, I am not much good."

Tara smiled at her. She noticed that Emily was playing with her empty ring finger. "You must miss your fiancé terribly," she said to Emily.

"I do," Emily nodded. It was hard not being able to talk to him. Because they were in the middle of the desert, it was not easy to get cell phone reception. They were, however, given the option to send letters. She had written letters to her fiancé but they probably took a long time to reach the U.S. The letters would have to be delivered to the capital city first and then flown to the U.S.

One of the passengers approached them. "I just saw some men riding out on horseback with weapons," she said to them. Tara and Emily looked at each other.

"Do you think they are going out into the desert?" Emily asked.

"I should think so."

Tara remained silent. She assumed that Sofian was making a move. She wanted to run and ask him about it but she had no idea where to find him. That could be an excuse for her to get inside his house. She was curious to see what it was like on the inside, if he had any photos and what kind of furniture he had. She was never going to be allowed in anyway. There were many guards. Also Sofian might be furious with her for the intrusion.

So she decided to linger around near his house but not too close. She hoped to catch him and she did. He approached her looking rather amused. "Are you stalking me?" he asked her. Tara made a face at him.

"I am certainly not," she snapped. He was so full of himself. Of course he would think that she was stalking him.

"Then what are you doing here? I am sure you still remember me telling you that this path leads to my home."

Tara had not thought it through. She had planned for it to look like they had bumped into each other but she had failed miserably.

The Sheikh's Girlfriend

"Do not flatter yourself. I just wanted to ask you if you sent men out into the desert," she said.

"What?"

"One of the passengers saw some men riding out."

"I have."

Tara felt both nervous and excited about it. "What is going to happen?" she asked.

"I am not going to divulge my plans to you. Good day." He walked past her and headed to his house. Tara followed him.

"Well, why not?" she asked. He turned to look at her and raised an eyebrow. Tara grinned at him in hopes to persuade him.

"Were they serving alcohol during lunch?" He could not recall a moment when Tara smiled at him. She narrowed her gaze at him.

"I am not drunk, just curious."

"As always."

"Sofian, just tell me," Tara cried out. She was getting frustrated with him.

"We are just checking out the situation first before we raid the place."

Tara nodded. "Was that so difficult to say?" she asked. Sofian laughed and walked off. Tara still followed. She was still curious to see his home. Tami was definitely going to be happy to hear about Sofian. She would be intrigued by the fact that he was a prince and actually had a residence in the desert. She would also want to know what it looked like on the inside. Sofian looked down at Tara and raised his eyebrow.

"Something else on your mind?" he asked her.

"You have a habit of walking off in the middle of the conversation," she replied.

"Were we still speaking?"

Tara narrowed her gaze at him. It annoyed her that he did not even realize that he had walked off without bidding her farewell. The conversation was dead anyway when he walked off but she was hoping to prolong it long enough for her to walk into his house and hopefully without him realizing.

Chapter 10

"Why did you not go with your men?" Tara asked. Of course as the prince he did not have to go but she had to keep the conversation going. They were almost at his house.

"I will go next time," he replied. The guards bowed to him as he approached. He came to a halt and looked at Tara. She stopped too.

"What?"

"Are you trying to get to into my house?"

Tara burst out laughing. She had been caught. She did not know that she was being obvious. "Since you're inviting me," she said.

"I wasn't," Sofian said lazily. Tara frowned at him. "If you must," he added and started walking. He was a little bit amused.

"Huh?" Tara was surprised. She had been expecting the opposite and thought that he would not let her in. She followed him into his house. She was curious and excited. One of the guards opened the door for them. Tara was pleasantly surprised when she saw the inside of the house. It was so modern. You would not guess it was in the middle of the desert.

The floors were dark Brazilian cherry wood. The ceilings were very high. There were steps leading upstairs on the left. The staircase was quite broad, and the railing was also made of Brazilian cherry wood. A maid came to greet the sheikh. She bowed to him and told him that lunch was ready. "Care to join me?" he asked Tara. She raised her eyebrows. "You might as well," he said to her and walked down the hallway. Tara followed behind him. The walls were white and paintings hung from them.

They walked into the dining room. The table was medium sized with a glass top. It was already set. Sofian sat down without pulling out the chair for Tara. "What a gentleman," she mumbled under her breath. But then again she had practically invited herself inside the house.

"What was that?" Sofian asked.

"You have a nice home."

"I know I do."

"You're welcome," Tara said sarcastically when he did not thank her. Sofian laughed. The maid served them lamb, tomato and green peas with rice. It looked and tasted much nicer than the food the passengers were served. Of course he would be served more delicious food since he was the sheikh. There was a selection of drinks; water, black tea, other teas that Tara could not recognize and cold beverages.

"The food is to your liking?" Sofian asked Tara. She nodded.

The Sheikh's Girlfriend

"Tastes good." She poured herself some water. "I am surprised you invited me in and for lunch," she added. He was surprised at himself also. He rarely allowed people into his home. He liked his privacy. He was getting soft, he thought to himself.

"Was I to leave you stranded at the door?"

Tara laughed. "I honestly thought you would," she said and took a sip from her glass. Sofian smiled in response. They ate lunch together and conversed a little. Tara had never been in Sofian's company for that long. She had mixed feelings about it. There were moments when she made eye contact with him. He held her gaze and did not look away. He had an intense gaze that made her stomach knot up.

After lunch, Tara asked to see the rest of the house. Sofian thought it was rather strange, since he had never been asked that before. People never asked the prince for such peculiar things or addressed him in such a casual manner.

"Seriously, Sofian, have you never given a tour before?" Tara asked when she noticed his facial expression. He looked confused. Tara tucked a stray lock of her blonde hair behind her ear. She had tucked most of her hair into a bun but some locks rested on her face and neck. Sofian had been watching them. He thought they were adorable.

The Sheikh's Girlfriend

Tara led herself back into the hallway and into the living room. It was quite large. The ceiling was quite high and there was a beautiful large chandelier hanging from it. The walls were so white. The sofas were red velvet with white cushions. There was a fluffy but expensive looking white rug in the center. Tara looked at everything as she walked around.

"I do not know if there is much to see," Sofian said hopelessly.

"There is plenty to see," Tara said as she slid the glass door to the right and walked out onto the green lawn. She gasped when she saw a swimming pool. She turned to face Sofian who was leaning in the doorway. "I bet you do not use it," she said. She could not picture Sofian swimming. He seemed so stiff. Swimming seemed too spontaneous for him.

"On the contrary, I do," he replied matter-of-factly.

"Really?" Tara looked amused.

"Why does that seem hard for you to believe?"

"Do you wear Speedos?" Tara laughed at the image of it.

"I wear nothing."

Tara stopped laughing and widened her eyes. Sofian was very serious. She had half expected him to say that he was joking. She opened her mouth to speak but then closed it. She was not even going to

The Sheikh's Girlfriend

challenge that answer. She walked towards him, back into the house. She blushed and avoided eye contact. She was still recovering from the image that had popped up in her mind because of his answer.

"Will you be off to my bedroom now?" Sofian asked. Tara whipped her head in his direction with a frown on her face.

"What?"

"It is just a question. I have no idea what exactly you want to see. So I am just asking if you wish to visit upstairs," Sofian answered so innocently. He could see that Tara was shocked by his question.

"Oh," Tara said and kept on walking. She headed upstairs to see the rest of the house. Sofian's bedroom was at the end of the hallway. Tara stopped and looked at Sofian before she walked in. She suddenly felt weird about it. She was about to walk into his bedroom.

"What?" he asked her.

"It just seems a little odd that I am about to make a spectacle of your bedroom."

Sofian shrugged his shoulders. "It was not odd before you came up?" he asked. Tara shook her head, he was rather clueless. She opened the door but did not walk in. She just looked from the doorway.

The Sheikh's Girlfriend

"Lovely," she said. The room was quite big. The best thing about it was the king-sized bed with lots of pillows. It looked so comfortable.

"You won't walk in?"

"No, I've seen enough, thank you."

"You are a peculiar woman."

Tara laughed. "I think you are just clueless," she said. Tara turned away to head back downstairs. She had seen most of his house and her curiosity had been satisfied. It was still odd to her that she had spent half of her afternoon with Sofian but his company was not bad.

Sofian escorted Tara downstairs and opened the door for her. He watched her walk out. She was very different from people he knew. Everything about her was just different but she was amusing and interesting. For once she had not irritated him. Was she growing on him? Sofian closed the door and headed back into his house. She could not possibly have been growing on him, at least not that quickly.

He hated to admit that lately she had been occupying his thoughts. He had mixed feelings about her. He could not understand himself when it came to her. It was rather odd that a normal girl would ask to see the sheikh's house, and yet he had allowed it. It did not bother him. He strangely found it nice to have her in his house. Sofian could still smell her perfume as he headed up to his room. She really did smell nice. The first time he had smelled her, was when he held her in his arms. Sofian grunted and dismissed the thoughts.

Chapter 11

Amir returned a few days later from the desert. He went straight to see the sheikh in his house. One of the sheikh's maids let Amir into the house and showed him to the sheikh. Sofian was sitting in his living room. Amir bowed to him before he sat down.

"Welcome back, friend," Sofian said to Amir.

"Thank you," Amir replied.

"So what happened?" Sofian was eager to find out what Amir had learned about the nomads. Amir nodded and started telling him what they had found out about the nomads. They had been able to conduct surveillance of El-Sadi village and the nomads' campsite without bringing attention to themselves. El-Sadi, the village on the border of Omani, was where the hostages were being kept.

"The hostages are to be used as brides," Amir said. Sofian's eyes flew open.

"What?" he shouted. "For whom?"

"The older rich men in the village or sheikhs from neighboring villages."

"That is preposterous!" Sofian felt anger wash over him. How could such a thing be happening?

"I agree, your highness."

The Sheikh's Girlfriend

Sofian stood up and started pacing. The maids were on their way in with tea and cakes but the sheikh dismissed them instantly. "We must rescue them at once!" he said. He could not bear the thought of telling Tara that her sister might be sold off to wed a stranger.

"Yes indeed, your highness. This cannot be left alone for any longer."

"This does not make sense. How can this be happening in this day and age?"

"There must be someone commanding the nomads."

"I want to see the man who would dare do this in my territory." Sofian was ready to tear someone's head off. He caught a glimpse of the swimming pool outside as he was pacing. It reminded him of Tara, when she asked him if he swam in it. The thought of her instantly calmed him down. He returned to his seat. "Do they have weapons?" Sofian asked.

"They do but not guns," Amir replied. He was little confused. The sheikh had been so angry a moment ago and then all of a sudden he was calm.

"Do they have many men?"

"We have more."

Sofian nodded. "We have to be prepared before go. We cannot afford to leave any hostages behind," he said.

The Sheikh's Girlfriend

"You will come?"

"Of course I will come."

Sofian wanted to find the man in charge of the nomads. They had to be taking orders from someone. He wanted to be the one who arrested the mastermind, the man responsible for kidnapping Tara's sister.

"I left a few men in the village to watch over the situation," Amir said. He had planted some spies in the village to find out more information, and then later relay it to him. Sofian told Amir to get the men ready. They were going to depart Wella City the following morning. Amir nodded and did as told.

Later that night, Sofian was dining by himself in his house. It suddenly felt strange to dine by himself. He had only dined with Tara once, and yet here he was thinking of her. He looked at the empty chair where she once sat. He felt as though he could still smell her. He remembered the many moments their eyes had locked.

"Excuse me, your highness," the maid said, interrupting his thoughts. He turned his head to look at her. She bowed her head to him. "There was a call from your mother," she said. Only his house and office had reliable signal. He was still working on getting better satellite service in Wella City so that everyone else could get signal. He had made it his mission to improve the city.

Sofian sighed before he responded. "What did she say?" he asked.

"She wanted to know when you will be returning to Iqbal City."

Sofian grunted. "If she calls again, which she will, tell her that I will return after I have dealt with the nomads," he said.

"Very well, your highness," the maid said but she still stood there. Her cheeks turned red.

"What is it?" Sofian asked her. He could see that she was feeling shy about something.

"There was a question of...a possible bride"

Sofian narrowed his gaze and kept eating his food. It was expected that his mother would enquire about it. She was impatiently waiting for him to wed. "You may go," he said to the maid. He was not going to say more on that matter.

After dinner, Sofian decided to take a walk. He told himself that he just wanted to clear his mind but deep down he knew that he hoped to run into Tara. He knew that she went on frequent walks. Maybe she was on another late walk. Sofian opened the front door and walked out into the night.

The Sheikh's Girlfriend

Sofian was frustrated and was almost about to give up. He had been walking for what felt like forever and there was no sign of Tara. That was much like her, he thought to himself. She always did the opposite of what she was meant to be doing. Just when he was about to return to his house, he heard someone address him in an impudent manner. "Sofian! What are you doing out here?" the person shouted. He already knew it was Tara. No one else would dare.

"None of your business," he replied as he turned to face her. She approached him.

"Are you looking for me?" she asked him.

"Why would I be?"

"Then why would you be around here?" He was near where the passengers were staying. Sofian cleared his throat when he realized how far he had come. He had been so consumed in his thoughts that he had not realized where he had walked to. He turned on his heel without responding to Tara and started heading back. Tara made a face and ran up to him. "Are you just going to return without saying what you came for?" she asked.

"I do not need to explain myself to you," he replied. He was not about to admit to her that he was indeed searching for her. Tara laughed. He was truly a complicated man.

"Whatever."

The Sheikh's Girlfriend

"I suppose you're out on one of your walks again."

"You suppose correctly."

They walked in silence for a while. No one knew where to start. Sofian had wanted to see her but he had not known what he was going to say her.

"Aren't you going to return to your room?" he asked, even though he did not want her to return. He needed to say something to fill the silence.

"You are awful at small talk." Tara had noticed that he often said awkward things or walked off when there was nothing to say.

"I have never needed to make small talk."

"And you have awful interpersonal skills."

"Are you going to keep pointing out my flaws?" he asked. He knit his eyebrows. "I did not even know I had any," he added. Tara looked at him and laughed sarcastically.

"Oh, you are so full of yourself."

"I am curious about one thing." He stopped walking and looked at Tara. "Why weren't you aware of my identity? Are you telling me that…Don't you watch news?" He had long wondered why she knew nothing about him and his family.

"Tami would know more about that stuff than me. She was into sheikhs and all that stuff. Partially the

The Sheikh's Girlfriend

reason why we came here. I don't really care for royals and all that. So obviously I would not know who you are nor would I care."

Sofian grunted. "Your sister seems smarter than you," he said.

"We have different interests."

"What exactly do you in the U.S.?"

"Are you asking for my occupation?" Tara widened her eyes. It was the first time he had asked about her life. She wondered where it was coming from. She looked up at the sky as if she was waiting for something. Sofian made a face.

"What are you doing?"

"Waiting for the sky to fall."

Sofian narrowed his gaze at her. Tara laughed and rubbed his shoulder. "Take a joke, will you. Anyway I work for a pharmaceutical company doing research for new medicine."

Sofian raised his eyebrows. "You? A scientist?"

"Why is that hard to believe?"

"Not really. Scientists are curious by nature. Makes sense now."

"What makes sense?"

"Your level of curiosity."

The Sheikh's Girlfriend

Tara narrowed her gaze. She was not that curious. He was the odd one. It was because he did not answer her properly. So she appeared very curious to him.

Chapter 12

Sofian was all of a sudden looking very serious. He looked down at Tara. Her dark blue eyes screamed innocence. She had her wavy locks down. She had not tied her hair up this time. Sofian wanted to touch her hair but he had to stop himself. "Tomorrow morning I will set off to the desert," he said.

"Why?" Tara asked.

"To find the hostages."

Tara's eyes widened. The time she had eagerly waited for had come. "Do you know where they are?" she asked. Sofian nodded. Tara started feeling nervous. She so badly wanted to see her sister and it seemed like she was going to be able to really soon. "How long will it take to get there? You're going by jeeps, right?" she asked.

Sofian smiled. She was back to herself, with the million and one questions. "Seven and a half hours," he said.

"That's a long time. How will you bring the hostages back?"

"I have arranged for them to be flown to Iqbal City instead of here."

"Then we meet them there?"

"Yes."

The Sheikh's Girlfriend

Tara blinked her tears away. She hoped that nothing had happened to her sister. Sofian touched her face. She let him touch her. He caressed her cheek with his thumb. "I will find her," he said to Tara. She found comfort in his words.

"What can I do to help?" Tara asked. She had always hated being useless. Sofian raised an eyebrow.

"Nothing, just stay here and not cause trouble," he said to her.

"I never cause trouble." Tara made a face at him. Sofian laughed a little.

"Believe it or not I am quite skilled in situations like this. I can handle it," said Sofian.

A subtle breeze blew Tara's hair back, revealing her beauty to Sofian. He raised his eyebrows. "What's wrong with you now?" Tara asked when she noticed his facial expression change.

"Why would there be something wrong?"

"Oh, you are weird. Conversation with you is weird." Tara shook her head.

"You are not making sense."

Tara sighed. "Just be safe and hurry back," she said. Sofian suddenly had a smirk on his face.

"I should hurry back?"

"Well of course. Do you want to stay there forever?"

The Sheikh's Girlfriend

"You worry for my safety."

Tara narrowed her gaze. He was really full of himself. "If you are harmed then you won't be able to help Tami. Seriously, Sofian, it's not always about you." She turned on her heel and walked off. Deep down she prayed for his safety. She did not want anything to happen to him.

Sofian smiled to himself as he watched Tara walk away. Her tone had suggested that he was correct. She really did worry for his safety but she was not going to admit it. He felt good after speaking to her, even though they had weird conversations; like she had said. He was not good at holding conversations with random people.

He was used to speaking with his family and giving orders to his men. Amir was probably one of the only people who wasn't family but spoke to the sheikh about anything. Therefore speaking to Tara was a challenge. She was always asking him a million questions and addressing him informally. Strangely it made him a more patient man.

Sofian returned to his house and headed straight to bed. He needed to rest well before heading off into the desert. They had a long journey ahead of them.

***

The next morning at breakfast, Mariam announced to the passengers that there had been a lead as to

The Sheikh's Girlfriend

where the hostages were being held. She told them not to worry and be patient. The sheikh was doing everything he could to rescue the passengers. Hae-Na looked at Tara. "It's good news," she said to her. Tara nodded. It was good to have good news at last.

"I do not want to get my hopes up but I feel a little bit excited," Jackie said. She had missed her daughter so dearly.

"I never thought they'd find them this soon," Emily said.

"I hope they really did find them," Mandy said. Tara was just sitting there quietly. After debating with herself whether or not to tell them, she finally came to a decision. Just as she was about to speak, she looked up and saw Hae-Na looking at her with a mischievous smile on her face.

"What?" she asked.

"What are you thinking about?" Hae-Na asked.

"I'm confused."

"Where were you last night?"

The other ladies looked at Tara. "I went for a walk, you know that," Tara said.

"She was gone for a while," Hae-Na said to the other ladies.

The Sheikh's Girlfriend

"Maybe she had a lot on her mind," Emily said in attempt to defend Tara. Hae-Na shook her head.

"A little birdie tells me that she met with a handsome fella."

They all looked at Tara suddenly wondering which fella Hae-Na was referring to. Tara scratched the back of her head awkwardly. "I went for a walk and we just ran into each other," she said.

"You and who?" Jackie asked.

"How do you know?" Tara asked Hae-Na.

"I did not until now," Hae-Na replied. Tara was confused. "You were gone longer than usual and you returned in a different mood. I suspected that you ran into each other but you just confirmed it now," she added. Tara dropped her jaw. She had been tricked and she fell for it.

"Who?" Emily asked.

"The sheikh." Hae-Na had a huge smile on her face.

"Is there something between them?" Emily asked. She had no clue as to what was going on.

"Yes."

"No!" Tara protested.

"Then what were the two of you speaking about for so long?"

"They know where the hostages are."

The Sheikh's Girlfriend

"What?" all the ladies said at the same time. They looked at her in shock. Tara nodded and put her coffee mug down. She told them everything from the beginning.

"He told you this yesterday?" Mandy asked. Tara shook her head.

"He told me from the moment they caught the nomads but I did not want to get your hopes up for nothing if they did not succeed in finding the hostages," she said. Jackie placed her hand on her heart.

"My God, they really will bring my little girl back," she said.

"I hope so," Tara said and took Jackie's hands into hers. Jackie smiled at her. She felt so emotional. It was the worst thing she had ever been through. She hoped that her daughter returned unscathed.

"But why did he keep you updated?" Emily asked. She was glad to be having her friends back but she was confused why Sofian had chosen to tell Tara all of this.

"My point exactly," Hae-Na said.

"Somehow we always ran into each other. I always asked questions and he sometimes gave answers," Tara replied.

"He could have chosen not to say anything about that," Hae-Na said.

"You are not helping," Tara complained. Hae-Na laughed in response. She had always felt that there was something between Tara and Sofian but Tara refused to acknowledge it.

"A man like that would not easily divulge sensitive information," Jackie said. Tara had not even thought that far. She was just glad that he was telling her.

"Maybe he felt bad for me because I was so worried about Tami."

"If that was the case then he would have told all of us," Mandy said.

"So all of you decided to gang up on me." Tara narrowed her gaze and shook her head. She bit into her pita bread. The subject at hand was making her feel uncomfortable.

"Do you feel something towards him?" Emily asked.

"No!" Tara cried out.

"Yes, she does," Hae-Na said. Jackie and Mandy started laughing at Tara.

"That reaction," Emily pointed out.

"We are changing the subject," Tara said. She kept on eating her food. She asked herself if she did like him. It was uncomfortable for her to think about it because she could not understand her feelings. They were all muddled up. No one had ever caused so much strife between her heart and head. He was one complicated man that turned her world upside down within weeks.

Chapter 13

Amir's spies greeted the sheikh and his men when they arrived in the village. They reported that they had found out where most of the hostages were being held. They were being kept at sheikh Hakim's home. The nomads took the hostages to his home, where they stayed until they were married off. Sofian was furious but not entirely surprised to learn that it was Hakim who was behind everything.

A year ago, Hakim had been released from prison. He had been embezzling money from the palace. When he was caught, he was demoted from his position and sent to prison for a few years. After he was released, he was banished from the city. He moved to El-Sadi. Everyone had assumed that he had moved there to repent. Sofian always had an inkling that he had held a grudge.

Sofian ordered his men to separate into groups. Some went with Amir to search the village. Others went with Sofian to Hakim's house to rescue the hostages being held there and to arrest Hakim. This time he was not going to be pardoned for his transgressions.

El-Sadi was not a very big village. The roads were dusty but developed enough to drive on. The houses were built out of different types of stone. A lot of the citizens rushed out of their homes when they heard the sounds of the cars. They stared as the jeeps drove by.

Sheikh Hakim's house was bigger than all the other houses. It was surrounded by a stone fence. The gate was made out of wood. Two of Sofian's men got out of the jeep and banged on the gate. A man opened the gate to see who it was. Sofian's men pushed him aside and opened the gate for the jeeps. The jeeps drove through the gates and into the yard. There were some nomads in the yard. They rushed to guard the house. They were caught off guard, so they did not have any weapons.

"Surrender now or get arrested," Sofian said to the nomads. Some of them looked at each other nervously. They wondered how the sheikh had found them. Some of them wavered. They did not want to be on the sheikh's bad side but it was already too late. They now had no choice but to fight. Their head ordered for them to attack. They rushed towards Sofian's men and started fighting.

Both sides threw fists towards each other. Sofian had instructed his men not to use guns unless it was necessary. He wanted all the nomads arrested and put in prison. Sofian ran up the concrete steps leading up to the house. He hit anyone that got in his way. He was in a rush to get into the house. The last man that was standing in his way dropped to his knees and surrendered. Sofian just walked around him and kicked the door open. As the door was closed, he had to kick it a few times before it flew open.

The maids screamed when they saw him walk into the house. Some of Sofian's men rushed in after him. They immediately started searching the house. There were a few guards in the house that tried to fight them off but Sofian's men were well trained.

"Where are the hostages?" Sofian asked the maids.

"Basement!" they screamed out. They were huddling together in fear.

"Calm down, I am not here to hurt you." Sofian was not going to hurt the women. "Where is Hakim?" he asked.

"He's not here," one of the maids replied.

"Where is he?"

"He left for Omar City with some hostages. He left just few minutes before you came."

Sofian cursed under his breath. He must have been on his way to sell some of the hostages. Sofian's men came up with some of the hostages. The hostages looked frightened. Sofian looked at them. He was thankful that they were unscathed but he was still angry that they were hostages in the first place.

"Don't be scared, we are here to help," Sofian said.

The Sheikh's Girlfriend

"Really?" one the hostages asked. Sofian nodded in response. He analyzed every hostage as they passed. None of them looked like Tara. For the life of him, he could not even remember her sister's name.

Omar City was a small city that was near El-Sadi but not in Omani. Sofian had to arrest Hakim before he left Omani. He took some of his men and left quickly. He left some to look after the hostages and take them to his planes. There was an open field where the planes could land. He had arranged for them to be flown to the city.

Sofian was fortunate to find Hakim in his car just before he left El-Sadi. Sofian's men surrounded Hakim and his men. "What is the meaning of this?" Hakim shouted. His eyes widened when he saw Sofian coming out of the car.

"That is exactly what I should ask you," Sofian replied as he walked towards Hakim's car. Hakim ordered his men to attack the sheikh. Some of them looked at him like he was crazy.

"He is the prince," one of the men said.

"And it will be a mistake to attack the prince. Besides I have more men than you," Sofian said. "Don't make me shoot you," he added. Hakim knew there was no point in trying to fight Sofian. He had already been caught and there was no way out.

The Sheikh's Girlfriend

"I have a gun," Hakim said desperately, as he searched the glove box of the car. He needed to get to Omar City and sell hostages. He had started robbing people and kidnapping women for money. He had lost money and status when he was arrested.

"Shoot me then." Sofian was not scared or intimidated. He kept walking towards Hakim.

"You think I will not shoot."

"Sheikh, it's over please," one of his men pleaded with Hakim. He knew that if Hakim shot the prince, then all of them would not be safe. "Think of your family," he added. Hakim groaned and dropped the gun.

When Sofian approached him, he punched him in the face. Hakim's head flew to the side. "Bastard," Sofian said. He ordered his men to help the hostages out of the cars and cuff the nomads. Sofian dragged Hakim out of the car and cuffed him. Fortunately, Amir arrived with the other men.

One of the hostages walked towards Hakim and slapped him in the face twice. Sofian raised his eyebrows and laughed. He did not blame her. She looked at him. "Thank you," she said. Sofian stared at her for a moment. She had long, wavy blonde hair. She had a golden skin tone. She was not that tall.

"You are Tara's sister," Sofian said. She raised her eyebrows.

The Sheikh's Girlfriend

"You know my sister? Is she okay?"

Sofian smiled. "She is fine."

"Oh, thank God." She sighed and placed her hands on her heart.

The hostages were flown to Iqbal City where the sheikh had arranged accommodation for them while they waited for the other passengers. The nomads spent the night in El-Sadi jail. Sofian's men guarded it so that no one escaped. They were to be taken to the city the following morning.

***

Sofian and his men arrived in Wella City the following night. It was already after dinner and most of the passengers had retired to their bedrooms. Sofian wanted to speak to Tara but he felt awkward about having to ask one of the staff members to search for her. He did not even know which room she slept in, so he could not go himself. He just went straight to his house.

His maids greeted him when he walked in. They asked to make him dinner but he refused. He went straight upstairs to have a shower. After taking a shower, he slipped into his silk pajama bottoms and a white tee shirt. He was just about to get into his bed when there was a knock on the door.

"Your highness, I hate to disturb you but there is a lady that seeks your audience," his maid said. Sofian

The Sheikh's Girlfriend

frowned. Before he could ask who it was, the door flew open and Tara walked in. "I tried to stop her but she insisted. So I let her in because you came with her before and–" the maid spoke so fast. Her voice was full of panic. Before she could finish speaking, Sofian cut her off.

"You may leave," he said to her. She bowed her head and left.

"I rushed over when I heard you were back," Tara said. She was still awake and about to go for a walk when she ran into some of the staff members. They had been talking about the sheikh's return.

"I knew you'd worry."

Tara rolled her eyes. "What happened? Did you find them?"

"Find who?"

"Sofian!" She was too anxious and he was not making it easy for her. He smiled and held her arms. She had the same look on her face as her sister. He had to hold her arms so that she did not slap him.

Chapter 14

"Relax, we found them all," Sofian said to Tara.

"Why did you not say that in the first place?"

"I am sorry," he said. Tara sighed with relief. Her eyes welled up. "I saw your sister," he added.

"What?" Tara knit her eyebrows.

"She looks just like you."

Tara gasped and jumped. "You saw her? Was she alright?" she asked.

"She was more than fine." Sofian remembered her slapping Hakim. She was just as bold as her sister. Tara threw her arms around Sofian. She was just so happy. Finally her sister was found and it was all thanks to Sofian. She did not know what she would have done without him. She released him from her embrace.

"Thank you so much."

"Are you that happy?" He wiped a tear from her eye with his thumb. Tara smiled.

"Yes, thank you so much, Sofian."

"I am unscathed, in case you were wondering."

Tara narrowed her gaze. "Well, you look fine. I did not need to ask," she mumbled. He was so full of

The Sheikh's Girlfriend

himself. She touched his cheeks. "Are you unharmed, your highness?" she asked sarcastically.

"You are an interesting woman." Most women would have been pampering him by now.

"I am joking with you. I really am glad that you are safe."

"Are you?"

"I am, really. I appreciate you."

Sofian raised his eyebrows. "You appreciate…ME?" He emphasized *me*. Tara opened her mouth. He never failed to take an opportunity to be conceited.

"I mean that–" Before she finished speaking, Sofian pulled her into his arms and pressed his lips against hers. He held her waist so gently as if she was fragile. Tara stood there for a moment, frozen with shock. She could not even think to protest or kiss him back.

Tara's lips were very soft. Sofian took his time kissing her. He gently caressed her back. The combination of Sofian's fingers on Tara's back and the touch of his lips made her knees buckle. She leaned on him and touched his arms. She slowly started responding to him. She kissed him back. When he broke off the kiss, Tara still stood there with her eyes closed. Sofian smiled and pressed another kiss on her lips.

The Sheikh's Girlfriend

He stared at her. She was so beautiful and he hated that it had taken him so long to admit it to himself. "I know what you mean," he said to her. Tara sighed with pleasure. She could not even remember what she was talking about. Sofian caressed her face. Her skin was so soft.

Tara smiled at him. "Good night," she said and left his room. She rushed downstairs and headed out of the front door. As soon as she was in the night, she placed her hand on her heart. It was racing so fast. She still could not grasp just exactly what had happened. She had to rush out of there. She was always so awkward in those intimate situations. "It's no wonder you are single," Tami would tease her.

No one had ever kissed her the way Sofian had. A few seconds in, and she was already going crazy with pleasure. She stumbled as she went back to her room. Her legs were still shaking. She stopped for a second to regain her breath. She closed her eyes and tried to calm herself down. Too much had happened within a space of an hour. She had learned that her sister was safe and been kissed by Sofian. It was too much to digest.

Tara woke Hae-Na up when she returned to their room. Hae-Na groaned as she turned to look at Tara. "What is it?" she asked her.

"Sofian is back, they found our people," Tara said. Hae-Na sat up instantly.

The Sheikh's Girlfriend

"What did you say?"

Tara smiled and nodded. "They were found and taken to Iqbal City."

"Oh my God!" Hae-Na screamed and jumped out of bed. She hugged Tara. She was so happy. The two of them rushed out of their room to go tell the other ladies. The other three were just as happy. Jackie started crying. Tara hugged her.

"My baby is safe," Jackie said.

"We get to see them soon," Emily said.

"I am so happy I could fly!" Hae-Na said.

The five of them stayed in Jackie's room talking until they fell asleep. They were all so overjoyed. It had been a nightmare not knowing what was going on with the hostages. It was now finally over.

The next morning, the good news of the hostages being found was given to the passengers over breakfast. The other passengers were also happy. Some of them were even crying. Mariam told the passengers to get their things ready as they were going to leave for Iqbal City that afternoon. It was unfortunate that their jewelry was not recovered, but the sheikh was going to give them some sort of compensation.

"Your lover is very generous," Hae-Na teased Tara.

The Sheikh's Girlfriend

"Not this again," Tara complained. "And he is not my lover!" she added.

"You were the first one to find out everything," Emily said and looked at her suspiciously. "Can you still say there is nothing between the two of you?"

"I went to him to find out. It is not like he looked for me."

"More excuses," Hae-Na said. Tara sighed. She honestly did not know what to make of their relationship if there was one. She sat there thinking about what was going to happen next. They were going to return to the capital city and be reunited with their loved ones. Then what? Go their separate ways and move on with their lives? Tara was not sure she could move on and pretend that nothing had happened. Just return to the U.S. and forget that she had ever met Sofian. He was not going to be easy to forget.

"What are you thinking about?" Mandy asked Tara.

"Just my sister. I can't wait to see her," Tara said.

"Let's go pack."

Tara nodded. They rose from their seats and went to their rooms to pack up their belongings. Mariam had said that they would be leaving at 1 o'clock. Transportation had already been organized.

The Sheikh's Girlfriend

***

Tara looked around before she got into the jeep. She was already feeling nostalgic. It dawned on her that she was never going to come to Wella City ever again. She had spent a month there. It felt like it was longer. It was different. In the U.S. she spent her days working, watching television, on the internet and going out with friends. In Wella City she did not have the distraction of technology. It was peaceful. The weather was great, the air was clean, the food was delicious and exotic, and then there was Sofian.

"Are you getting in?" Hae-Na asked.

"I am going to miss this place," Tara said.

"Strangely so will I."

Tara got into the jeep and shut the door behind her. The good thing was the drive was going to take three hours. She could not bear a long journey. She was too excited to see her sister. She made eye contact with Sofian as he was getting into his jeep. She smiled at him and he smiled back at her. Tara started remembering the night before, when he kissed her. She felt shy just thinking about it.

Chapter 15

The passengers finally reached Iqbal City. They arrived at some hostels, where the hostages were accommodated. They were already waiting outside for the passengers. Tara caught a glimpse of her sister, she rushed out of the car and ran towards her. Tami also ran towards her sister. They hugged as soon as they approached each other.

"Tami, you are safe," Tara said as she squeezed her baby sister too tightly. She had been so sick with worry. "I missed you so much."

"I missed you too," Tami replied.

"Did they hurt you in any way?"

"No."

"Are you sure?" Tara pulled Tami out of her embrace and analyzed her to make sure every part of her was intact. Tami laughed.

"I am fine, I swear."

Tara hugged Tami again and kissed her forehead. "I am glad," she said.

Sofian was leaning on his jeep watching Tara being reunited with her sister. It made him smile to see her so happy. He could see that she really cared for her sister. The way she had talked about her so much in the past month and how happy she was after being reunited with her. Sofian could see that Tara was a good person. It made him sad to know that she was going to return to the U.S. It felt too soon to let her go.

Tara and Tami went to speak with Sofian. He watched them walking towards him with big smiles on their faces. It was a little strange for him to see Tara smiling so much. "I have to thank you once again," Tara said to Sofian as soon as she approached him. He smiled at Tara and nodded. Their smiles faded but they still stared at each other. Neither one of them looked away. Tami was starting to feel awkward. She cleared her throat.

"I'm Tami, Tara's younger sister as you already knew," she introduced herself.

"Oh, sorry, Tami," Tara said and broke off the eye contact.

"Hello, Tami," Sofian greeted her.

"This is Sofian. He's a sheikh."

Tami's eyes widened. She had always wanted to meet one. "What?" she called out at the top of her lungs. She looked him up and down. "As in Prince Sofian Botros?" she asked. Tara whipped her head in Tami's direction and frowned.

"Even your sister knows me," Sofian said to Tara. Tara just shrugged her shoulders. It was not important to her.

"I thought you looked familiar but I could not put my finger on where I knew you from," Tami said and gasped. She looked at Tara with her eyes widened. "What are the odds that we meet a prince?" she asked.

"Yes, what are the odds?" Tara asked sarcastically. Sofian was just analyzing the two of them. They both had golden tans, but Tami was a shade lighter than Tara and she was slimmer. She had more of a pear-shaped body and Tara had an hourglass figure. They both had long blonde hair that fell in waves. They both had oval-shaped faces. They were the same height.

"My sister can be a bumpkin at times," Tami joked. Tara laughed and shoved her playfully.

"So where are you going now? Back to Wella City or to the palace?" Tara asked.

"I will call on my mother and then I will go to my own house," Sofian replied.

"You do not live in the palace?" Tami looked at Tara like she had asked a stupid question. "What?"

"No, he does not live in the palace," Tami said to Tara like it was something obvious. Tara shrugged her shoulders. Well, how was she to know? Sofian laughed a little. Watching them together was like watching a comedy.

"Where will the two of you go?" Sofian asked.

The Sheikh's Girlfriend

"Continue with the rest of our vacation. I still have yet to see Omani and actually enjoy my graduation present," Tami said. Tara sighed. She needed to call her work back in the U.S. She had been gone for longer than she told them. They also needed to sort out their accommodation, see if they could still stay at the hotel they had booked or get a refund. Tara was always wondering where to go and what to do.

"We can only stay few days anyway," Tara said. They did not have much money to stay longer.

"If you need anything, feel free to speak to Mariam," Sofian said. She was helping the other passengers that needed money or accommodation or transportation.

"Thanks," Tara said.

"We won't see you again?" Tami asked. Tara was glad that her sister asked because she too was curious but did not know how to ask.

"You will. I will bid you farewell before you leave," Sofian said.

"You don't know where we are staying," Tara said. Tami narrowed her gaze at her.

"I am sure he could find any one in Omani at the snap of his finger."

Tara rolled her eyes. "My sister is too much of your fan," she said.

The Sheikh's Girlfriend

"I will see you soon," Sofian said to Tara and shook her hand. He was awkward at such situations. He wanted to pull her into his arms and kiss her but he did not. There was something about Tara that threw him off his game. He never had to work hard to get a woman in his life. They all threw themselves at him but Tara did not. And it confused him.

Sofian just held her hand in his and stared at her. Tara stared back at him. The feeling of his strong but soft hands made her stomach knot. She could still remember the feeling of his hands on her back and her face. She wanted to kiss him but she was not bold enough. When it came to relationships and men, she was so clueless.

Sofian looked at her full lips and lifted his gaze slowly until he was looking at her eyes again. He wanted to kiss her. He still remembered the feeling of her lips, the taste of them. Not being able to kiss them once more drove him crazy. In that moment, it felt like it was just the two of them. He had forgotten where they were until he heard Amir speak.

Tami was just standing there watching them and feeling like a third wheel. Sofian was not even sure what Amir had said or when he had come. "They have been like this for like a minute now," Tami said. She felt like it had been longer. Tara pulled her hand away and looked at Amir.

The Sheikh's Girlfriend

"Hello, Amir," she said and smiled. "I need to thank you also," she added.

"Don't," he said and smiled at her. He kissed her on both cheeks. "I wish you the best of luck. Feel free to call if you need anything. I have instructed Mariam to give you my contact details."

"That is nice of you," Tara said. She took Tami's hand. "Bye," she said to Amir and Sofian. As they were walking away, Tara turned to look at Sofian. He was still looking at her. She smiled and looked away.

"You gave Mariam your details?" Sofian asked Amir. He did not understand why his friend had done so. He had only spoken to Tara on a few occasions.

"No, I gave her yours," Amir replied as he walked away.

"What?"

"I knew you wouldn't. You're welcome"

Sofian shrugged his shoulders and walked off. His friend knew him too well. He headed to his car. His driver had come to pick him up. He greeted Sofian with a bow and opened the car door for him. Sofian got into the car. The driver shut the door and then got in at the driver's seat, and then they were off.

Tara needed to say goodbye to her tent mates. Some of the passengers had already left after being reunited

The Sheikh's Girlfriend

with each other. Tara hugged Hae-Na and introduced Tami to her. Hae-Na introduced her friend to Tara.

"So…Sofian?" Hae-Na asked.

"What about him?" Tara asked.

"Is that it? You go your separate ways?"

"What else?"

"You should have been there to see it," Tami said to Hae-Na. "There were moments where they just stared at each other and said nothing."

Hae-Na's eyes widened. Tara closed her eyes. It was bad enough that Hae-Na had been on her case since the beginning, and now her sister was in on it. "He probably wanted to kiss her," Hae-Na joked.

"I think if I was not there, they would have."

"Hi, girls," Jackie said as she approached them. Tara was so happy that she had interrupted at the perfect moment. Emily and Mandy approached moments later. Tara and the ladies swapped their contact details. They were definitely going to meet up when they returned to the U.S. For now they were going their separate ways. They hugged each other before they did so. Tara felt sad to be parted from them. They had formed strong bonds with each other in such a short time.

Chapter 16

A few days later, Sofian went to the palace to see his mother. She had called him over for some afternoon tea. He kissed her on both cheeks before he sat down at the table with her. She asked him about the nomads. He told her that they had been sentenced to a few years in prison, except for Hakim, who had been sentenced to life because he was the mastermind. He had kidnapped so many people and stolen from them. On top of that he had been selling them off. Sofian had notified the authorities in the neighboring countries so that they could search for the men that were buying these women.

"Oh my, you have been busy," his mother said. Her maid walked in with three women. They bowed their heads to Sofian before they sat down.

"Who are they?" Sofian asked his mother.

"Aren't they beautiful?" she asked him. Sofian narrowed his gaze. He already knew where she was going with it.

"Why?"

"Introduce yourselves," his mother said to the women.

"My name is Zara," the first one spoke and bowed her head to Sofian. He stared at her with an unfriendly gaze as she spoke. She was so stiff. She had jet-black hair, olive-colored skin and high cheekbones.

He scanned the three of them. Tara was much better looking than them. She had more character and was far more interesting. It was weird not seeing her any more. It was more than weird, it was hard. The last few nights, he had barely gotten some sleep. He even took a walk into his garden the night before but it was not the same. It was as if he always took late nights with Tara. Walking alone was boring and strange.

He regretted not kissing her the same time that he had seen her, when they arrived in Iqbal City. His lips were aching to touch hers once more. He wanted to touch her body. Suddenly the thought of her having a boyfriend came to him. It made him angry. What if she was seeing someone in the U.S.? He shook his head. She could not possibly have someone, otherwise she would not have kissed him. Jealousy and fury washed over him in waves. He could not survive the thought of her in another man's arms.

"Sofian!" His mother called out. He turned to look at her. "What is it that is making you this angry? Are the girls not to your liking?" she asked. She had noticed him sitting there not saying anything and then his expression changing into a dark one.

"No they are not," he said. They were not Tara.

The Sheikh's Girlfriend

"Then tell me what you are looking for in a woman. I will find her for you."

"Don't." Sofian stood up and kissed his mother on the cheek. Then he walked off. She was left sitting there speechless. She could not grasp what exactly had just happened. It was not the first time she brought women over for him but this was the first time that he had reacted that way.

Sofian went to see Amir at his home. He was the only one who could understand Sofian's thoughts. He needed to speak with him immediately. Amir was in his living room reading a newspaper. He raised his eyebrows when his maid announced the sheikh's arrival. Sofian walked in and sat on the sofa.

"What brings you over?" Amir asked. He could see that Sofian looked a little bit unsettled.

"I am losing my sanity," Sofian replied. He had never felt that strongly about anyone. He could not understand his feelings.

"Because of what?"

"Tara."

"Of course." Amir smiled.

Sofian sighed before he spoke. "My mother summoned me to the palace so that I could pick a bride."

Amir raised his eyebrows. "Again?"

"She is very tenacious."

"So what does this have to do with Tara?" Amir asked

"They are nothing like her. No one is!" Sofian rubbed his face. Amir was enjoying himself. He had never seen Sofian be flustered and unsettled because of a woman. "You've seen her, she is not my type."

"That is the point."

"Point of what?"

"The one you fall in love with is usually different from your past lovers."

"Who's in love?"

Amir started laughing. The maid brought in some tea and sweet pastries. She poured tea for them before she left the room. Amir picked up a slice of *basbousa* and ate it. "Sheikh, what exactly do you feel for this girl? No, I don't think you have actually figured it out. Otherwise you would not be here," Amir said as he picked up a cup of tea.

"I can't stop thinking about her. It is ludicrous. It is at the point where I am not sleeping very well," Sofian said. He picked up his cup and took a sip. He frowned and put it back on the tray.

"The reason is so obvious and yet you miss it."

The Sheikh's Girlfriend

"I have never met a woman who could unravel me," Sofian sighed.

"I told you she was charming."

Sofian frowned at Amir. "If that's what you want to call it," he said. Amir chuckled.

"So what are you going to do about it?" he asked.

"I do not know. That is why I am here."

Amir shook his head. Sofian was a very intelligent man. He was good at everything he did except in relationships. He was hopeless with women especially because he had never had a proper relationship. Nothing lasted longer than a week or two for him. He did not understand women. He never had to look for them. Most single women in Omani wanted to be with him. The married ones dreamed of being with him. "I must say it is amusing to see a woman affect you this much," Amir said as he ate his *basbousa*. Sofian shook his head.

"You are enjoying this too much."

"Go talk to her."

"And say what?"

"You will figure it out."

Sofian grunted. He got up to his feet. "You are bad at giving advice and your tea does not taste good," he said as he turned on his heel and headed for the exit. Amir smiled to himself.

***

Tara was lying on the floor ignoring the pile of clothes next to her. It was time for them to pack up. They were flying back in two days. She was not bothered with the packing as she always left it till last minute; Tami always did things in advance. Tara was happy to have her sister back and it was fun seeing what Omani had to offer but she missed Wella City. She missed her tent mates and she missed Sofian. He was hard to speak to but she felt that she was starting to understand him.

"Tara, get up and pack," Tami said as she walked into the bedroom. They had been staying at a hotel in a double room with two beds.

"Later," she said. Tami shook her head. She knew that Tara was just going to pick up the clothes and throw them in the suitcase. That was her version of packing.

"Have you called Amir?"

"What for?"

"He gave you his number, didn't he?"

"Yes, I will call tomorrow to thank him and say goodbye."

"He is handsome though, isn't he?"

The Sheikh's Girlfriend

Tara snorted as she remembered Hae-Na practically drooling over him. "He is," she said.

Chapter 17

Sofian frowned when his phone rang. He pulled it out of his pocket and looked at the screen. He did not recognize the number. "Hello," he answered lazily.

"H…hello?" the person on the phone spoke.

"Who is this?" he asked.

"Tara."

There was silence for a moment. "It's Sofian," he said.

Tara gasped. Her heart dropped and almost exploded out of her chest. "Isn't this Amir's phone?" she asked.

"No, it's mine."

Tara was confused but it was good to hear his voice again. It was so deep and refined. She sat down on the sofa and just held the phone. She could not say anything. Sofian was not speaking either. Tami walked past Tara with a raised eyebrow. "Are you on hold?" she asked Tara. Tara did not reply.

"Open your door," Sofian said.

"What?" Tara asked.

"Now."

Tara got up and walked over to the door. She dropped her phone when she saw Sofian standing there. He put his phone in his pocket. He wrapped his arms around Tara and kissed her. She responded immediately. She wrapped her arms around his neck. Tami was just standing with her jaw hanging open.

"What are you doing here?" Tara asked him. He walked into the room and shut the door behind him.

"Well that was epic," Tami said.

"Hello, Tami," Sofian greeted her. Tara crossed her arms over her chest. She was half annoyed with him for not coming any sooner or even calling.

"Hi."

"You only come now," Tara said to him.

"You were waiting for me," Sofian replied.

"No," she lied. Sofian looked at her legs. She was wearing shorts and a tee shirt.

"I have never seen your legs."

Tara very rarely showed her legs. She immediately started feeling shy when Sofian pointed them out. "I'll go change," she said.

"Don't," Sofian replied, still looking at her legs. Tami opened her mouth and then closed it. If there was another room, she would have walked out. It was very awkward to be around Sofian and Tara.

"We leave tomorrow morning," Tara said. It cut her up to say it because she could not imagine a world where Sofian did not exist.

"Don't go."

"What?" Tara was confused. Tami gasped and placed her hand on her chest. She sat down on the bed.

"Stay here."

"Stay where?"

"In Omani."

"Why?"

Tami rolled her eyes. Her sister was impossibly slow when it came to guys. Sofian was not making it any easier for her either. He was not romantic. He did not know the right words to say.

"Because if I let you go, I'll never be the same again," he said.

"How so? Sofian, make sense," Tara said.

"Are you in a relationship?"

Tami slammed her face into her palm.

"What? No, why?" Tara frowned.

"Good, the thought of you with another man kills me. So stay here in Omani with me."

"Sofian…" Tara was speechless. Sofian reached into his pocket.

"In the past few days, I could not do anything without you jumping into my thoughts. This morning I was thinking of you and then I found myself

The Sheikh's Girlfriend

holding this." He pulled a little sachet out of his pocket. He opened it and pulled out a ring. The band was gold and it had a large blue sapphire in the middle and two diamonds on each side. Tami gasped and covered her mouth with her hands.

Tara stared at the ring with her eyes widened. Her heart was beating at a hundred miles per second. A million thoughts started rushing through her head. She had already been so cut up about leaving him. She had never felt the way she did about any man the way she did for Sofian. He was arrogant and full of himself but he was a good man. He went above and beyond for his people. She had enjoyed spending time with him in Wella City. She hated that it had taken her too long to admit it.

"This belonged to my grandmother," he said to her. He dropped to one knee. "I have never knelt before anyone but I will kneel and beg if it means you will stay with me and be my wife."

Tara laughed. "This is crazy," she said. There was nothing for her to return to in the U.S. No parents, no family, there was no Sofian.

"Well?" Tami asked impatiently. She was waiting for her sister to answer. Tara had told her everything that had happened between herself and Sofian. Tami already knew that they were in love with each other. She had felt the connection between them and it was strong. She had never seen her sister look at anyone the way she looked at Sofian.

Tara nodded. "Yes, I'll be your wife," she said. Sofian sighed with relief. He had been feeling so nervous about it. It was the hardest thing he had ever done in his life. He slipped the ring on her finger and it fit like a glove.

"Yes!" Tami cried out and jumped up to her feet. She rushed over to them and hugged them. Sofian laughed.

"You realize that this is meant to be a moment for two people?" Tara said to her.

"I was quiet for the most of it. It's finished now."

Tara laughed and hugged her sister.

"So you two love each other right? Because you still haven't said it," Tami added. Tara raised her eyebrows.

"Yes," Sofian said. "I love her much more than either one of us could understand."

"This is great! If you said no to her, I was not going to let you live," Tami said. Tara smiled. It was so typical of Tami.

***

Sofian moved Tara and Tami into his home. Tami was also going to stay in Omani with Tara. She had

The Sheikh's Girlfriend

always wanted to travel in the Middle East countries anyway. She did not mind staying. Tara and Sofian decided to sleep in separate rooms until they had wed. Tara wanted to stay a virgin until their wedding night.

Sofian invited his family to come to his house that weekend. He wanted to introduce Tara and Tami to them.

Amir was the first one to arrive. He greeted Tara and Tami. "You both look lovely," he said to them. They were both wearing long cocktail dresses. Tara was in blue and Tami was in green. Amir went to greet Sofian.

"I said figure it out and you asked her to marry you," he said to Sofian.

"I just came to that decision moments before I went to see her," Sofian replied.

Amir smiled. "Now can you admit that you love her?"

Sofian laughed. "I love her," he said. He had never said those words and yet they flowed out so easily where Tara was concerned.

"I am happy for you. She is a great woman."

Sofian's family arrived moments later. His mother was dressed elegantly as usual with her pearl necklace and earrings. Her hair was pinned up. She looked quite young for a woman whose first son was forty.

The Sheikh's Girlfriend

Sofian's older brothers had come also. They were dressed in suits. His father had passed away years ago. That was when his older brother inherited the throne.

"That's the king," Tami whispered to Tara. She knew that her sister would not know. "The one with the side parting in his hair," she added.

"They're all handsome," Tara said.

"I know, right."

Sofian took Tara's hand. Before he could introduce her to the family, his mother recognized the ring on her finger. She gasped. "Finally," she said and approached Tara. She kissed on her both cheeks.

"Mother?" Sofian said.

"She is wearing your grandmother's ring. Finally you are engaged. I thought you were going to introduce your wife to my grave," she said.

"So dramatic," Sofian said and shook his head.

"What is your name?" she asked.

"Tara."

"And she is beautiful too." His mother was so happy that her son was finally engaged. Sofian's brothers also greeted Tara. Sofian also introduced Tami to them. "We have a lot to catch up on," his mother said to Tara and Tami. She was eager to get to know them and especially how Tara had managed to capture Sofian's heart.

Epilogue

Tara stared at herself in the mirror. She was the girl that was always single, now here she was in a wedding dress and getting married to a prince. It was like a fairy tale, even though she had not believed in fairy tales. Tara sighed. She wished her mother could have been there to see her. Tami stood behind her sister and wrapped her arms around her waist.

"You look beautiful," Tami said to her.

"For once I believe you," Tara said and smiled. She loved the way the strapless wedding dress shaped her curves. The dress was tight-fitting. It had gold embroidery at the sides. Her wavy hair was blow-dried straight and pinned up. Her white lace veil was fastened into her hair. She wore white peep-toe heels with a platform front and red soles.

Sofian's mother had helped Tara pick out her wedding dress. In fact she had also done the planning for the wedding. Tara would have been fine with an intimate wedding but his mother insisted. She wanted to have a big, elaborate, sophisticated wedding. She wanted everyone to witness her son finally getting married and she also wanted to show off her new daughter-in-law.

"It is kind of sad that there are no parents on my side," Tara said just before they walked out of the room.

The Sheikh's Girlfriend

"We have each other and that is enough. I will give you away," Tami said and then hugged her sister from the side. "Are you ready to marry your prince?" she asked.

Tara nodded. "Yes, today is the happiest day in my life."

"Let's go then."

About Kate Goldman

In childhood I observed a huge love between my mother and father and promised myself that one day I would meet a man whom I would fall in love with head over heels. At the age of 16, I wrote my first romance story that was published in a student magazine and was read by my entire neighborhood. I enjoy writing romance stories that readers can turn into captivating imaginary movies where characters fall in love, overcome difficult obstacles, and participate in best adventures of their lives. Most of the time you can find me reading a great fiction book in a cozy armchair, writing a romance story in a hammock near the ocean, or traveling around the world with my beloved husband.

One Last Thing…

If you believe that *The Sheikh's Girlfriend i*s worth sharing, would you spend a minute to let your friends know about it?

If this book lets them have a great time, they will be enormously grateful to you – as will I.

Kate

www.KateGoldmanBooks.com

In Love With a Haunted House

The last thing Mallory Clark wants to do is move back home. She has no choice, though, since the company she worked for in Chicago has just downsized her, and everybody else. To make matters worse her fiancé has broken their engagement, and her heart, leaving her hurting and scarred. When her mother tells her that the house she always coveted as a child, the once-famed Gray Oaks Manor, is not only on the market but selling for a song, it seems to Mallory that the best thing she could possibly do would be to put Chicago, and everything and everyone in it, behind her. Arriving back home she runs into gorgeous and mysterious Blake Hunter. Blake is new to town and like her he is interested in buying the crumbling old Victorian on the edge of the historic downtown center, although his reasons are his own. Blake is instantly intrigued by the flame-haired beauty with the fiery temper and the vulnerable expression in her eyes. He can feel the attraction between them and knows it is mutual, but he also knows that the last thing on earth he needs is to get involved with a woman determined to take away a house he has to have.

A Dream for Two

Elise Roberts dreams of being a pop star but has been stuck in her hometown since she graduated from high school. Her life seems achingly dull and mapped out when she's suddenly laid off from the offices where she works as a secretary. With her faithful guitar Elise moves to New York where she takes up waitressing but sings at open mic nights. One night she meets the charismatic Dylan, who is the lead singer for his up-and-coming band. Dylan oozes charm but also arrogance and Elise initially dislikes him. As they vie for attention each night on the same open mic circuit, they come into conflict with one another, but beneath this conflict they harbor more intense feelings for one another. Just as Elise and Dylan have fallen head-over-heels in love, their dreams come true and each of them strikes a deal with a famous record label. Now they are being torn apart by their careers and begin to question whether their success is worth anything if they are not together. Can Dylan and Elise's new love survive the strain of their burgeoning careers and is either of them willing to sacrifice their dream for the sake of their relationship?

Love for Dessert

When Anastasia Emmott learns of her best friend's engagement, she hopes that her own boyfriend of three years will propose. But instead of giving her a ring, he breaks her heart by leaving her for another woman two weeks before their anniversary. If that wasn't bad enough, Anastasia receives news that she may be demoted to a terrible position in her accounting firm. She decides that finally, she needs change in her life. She quits her job and, much to the chagrin of her mother, starts up her very own bakery. After several disastrous dates, Anastasia begins to realize that the dating game is much harder than it used to be. But when Anastasia's best friend, Ariana, pushes her to enter a baking contest, she meets Darren King, a handsome baker who has just started at the competing bakery across the street. Anastasia is swept away by his dashing good looks, charming personality and masterful baking skills. What Anastasia doesn't know is that Darren is an undercover agent, planted in the bakery to gather evidence against a drug kingpin that has been operating out of his bakery. When Anastasia becomes involved by accident and her name is put on the hit list of the city's biggest drug gang, there is no one but Darren to save her.

Printed in Dunstable, United Kingdom